Keyboardist Sam Roland and her rock band, Approaching Grace, sit poised to break into the big leagues.

When Sam purchases a damaged tour bus, she discovers another band on board: Stadium, the 80s metal group that inspired Approaching Grace.

Stadium, who died in a bus crash forty years ago.

But can Sam and the other members of Approaching Grace learn the hard lessons from Stadium before fame rips them apart?

Get ready for one wild rock-and-roll ride.

Ghost Writers
Hailey Ezzell

ISBN 978-1-946462-26-8

Cover art: © Hailey Ezzell
Cover design: Noah Pritchard and Haley Jacobs
Editing and interior design: Dayle Dermatis

Ghost Writers

Prologue

Northwest Regional Library was not a place that Sam had been before. She had never even been in the city of Coral Springs, Florida, but as she looked out from behind a curtain at the swarm of people settled on the tacky, geometrically decorated carpet, she felt she had made the right choice to hold the book signing here. Besides, it held a deeper meaning than most probably realized. *The guys always told me about this place, but I never expected it to be so...normal. They always described it like magic.* The people in front of her varied greatly in age and ethnicity, from one woman in her seventies to a young man holding a baby that possessed the biggest puff of kinky black hair that Sam had ever seen. A good majority of the crowd sported band shirts, either from her solo career or the old band. Sam smiled. *All these people are here for me. It's like nothing I could've ever imagined.* Scanning the crowd, almost frantically, it took a moment for her to spot them—a group of four eccentrically dressed men, in animal prints and leather and doused in so much hairspray that one could almost taste it in the air. They stood surrounded in a cloud of smoke, but no one around them seemed bothered by this at all.

Nobody even noticed. The men looked at her, each wearing a wide grin that Sam acknowledged with a quick nod.

A tall woman with even taller heels and a head of freshly curled brown hair walked out from between rows of dusty books and towards the plain gray curtain Sam was standing behind. Pulling her handheld microphone away from her mouth, the woman spoke, "Are you ready, Ms. Roland?"

"I think so, Carla." She attempted to put her at ease, using her own feigned comfort, but the effect was unsuccessful.

Carla's tight smile grew even stiffer as she walked in front of the curtain and onto the stage, which was really just a tape outline on the carpeted floor, and raised the microphone to her lips. "Ladies and gentlemen, we have a very special guest at our library today. She's a four-time platinum-selling artist, a three-time Grammy Award–winning performer, and now, a *New York Times* bestselling author for her new memoir, *Ghost Writers*. Everyone, please welcome Samantha Roland!" The large crowd exploded into a cacophony of cheers, clapping, and yelling as Sam walked out and offered an open-handed wave to the crowd. Before she could sit down behind the brown school table, Carla handed her the microphone and quickly skittered off the "stage" and back between aisles of books, leaving Sam alone with the crowd.

"Afternoon, everybody," Sam said, sitting back down behind the school desk. The crowd ate it up, continuing to cheer voraciously. *You'd think I was stripping up here or something. Though, I'm not twenty anymore, so I'm not sure they'd be into that. Actually, I'm sure someone would be.* Her eyes shot to the back at the room again and smirked at the men there. *They're all still here. Good. I wonder how long that will last.* She frowned for a moment, her eyes falling to the floor, before darting back to the group again. The tallest one, a man with a mop of brown hair, pulled her out of her mental spiral by telling her to "speed up" with a quick circular movement of his finger. *Get out of your head, Roland. You're in front of an audience, just like a show. Focus, dammit.* She sat up a bit straighter and reached for the hardcover book that sat on the left side of the table.

Thank God for Blades. She saw him nod encouragingly, and she took a deep breath, "Thank you all for coming out today. It really warms my heart to see you here." The crowd got quiet, attentively listening to her every word. Sam looked at the cover of the book and smiled at the two photos on it: a photo of a younger Sam with her three bandmates, and a Polaroid photo containing the four men from the back of the room. "As a child, I always wanted to be one of two things; either a rock star or a writer. Now, at forty years old, I can say that I have become both and it is all because of you guys." She paused, looking up from the book cover to address the crowd. "What we're doing right now would make my younger self so happy." Sam's smile widened. "For those of you who don't know, *Ghost Writers* is a book that I wrote about the history of my band, Approaching Grace, and the connections that we have with the notorious eighties hair band Stadium. Those of you familiar with Stadium will recall their tragic demise in a tour bus accident early on in their career, but you may not know that Stadium was actually formed here in Broward County. Two of the band members, Ronnie and Mark, met in this very library, which is why I thought it would be more than appropriate to hold this event here today."

Ronnie and Mark, upon hearing their names, started clapping, making the smoke surrounding them dance and wiggle in the air. Ronnie put his fingers in his mouth and let out a long whistle. Sam chuckled softly, trying to keep herself under control as she looked back at the people in the crowd, unaware of the mischief occurring right under their noses. The baby Sam had seen earlier started to cry and her father quickly set about trying to calm the child. *Children and dogs,* Sam thought. She shook her head lightly, trying to get back on track.

"But enough history, we can get to all of that in the book. You know how this works, right?" Not pausing to allow the rambunctious crowd any time to respond, Sam said, "I'm going to read a good ol' lengthy section from my book and then there will be an opportunity for questions and autographs. That work for you?" Sam asked. The crowd, apparently worn out from their strong start, offered a relaxed cheer. "All right. Now, if you don't mind me," Sam started, leaning to retrieve her reading glasses from her purse, "I forgot to put in contacts today, so you get to see my 'secret' glasses."

She slid the glasses over her blue eyes just as she saw a young girl take a photo out of the corner of her eye. With her glasses secured on her face, Sam made eye contact with the girl. *Caught ya.* Sam smiled and the girl blushed a deep red and attempted to hide behind a veil of dark brown hair. *So much like Amy....* "If you go upstairs afterwards and print that photo out, I will sign it, okay?" Sam told her and the girl nodded enthusiastically, blush fading as a smile spread across her face, revealing a shiny set of braces.

"Okay. Let's start at the beginning, shall we? This is *Ghost Writers* by Samantha Roland. Hey, that's me!" A few people chuckled lightly at her joke and she cracked open the book, flipping through ten pages of filler before finding it. "Here we are. 'Chapter 1: Dreams.'" She scanned the crowd and let out a selfish sigh of relief upon seeing that the four men were still in their same spot. They had yet to vanish. Shaking her head at herself and her inevitable fate, Sam finally started.

"'My mother had always called me a big dreamer. I didn't know, at the time, that that could be taken a few different ways....'"

Dreams

My mother had always called me a big dreamer. I didn't know at the time that this could be taken a few different ways. Some people are dreamy in the way that their head is always in the clouds; they create these magical faraway worlds and play in them for hours. Others are dreamers in the way that they often can't focus on the task at hand. Yet another group are dreamy in the sense that they have what others would deem to be unrealistic expectations for their lives. And I was in the middle of this Venn diagram.

In school, I found I could only really focus in art or music class. That was when I truly became myself. With no right or wrong answers, I had the freedom to do what I wanted to do. As long as there was paint on the canvas or a sound coming out of the xylophone, my teachers would be happy. And I'll admit it now—I've always been a person who thrives on praise, and the praise that I received from my attempts at art both worked to fill that desire for approval and a personal need to create. So, I chose this path early in life.

Around middle school, I dropped the art aspect and began to focus on music. I had started taking piano lessons in elementary school, but now I was bastardizing them by fore-going Beethoven for Bon Jovi. It was around this time that I met Amy. I didn't realize then, sitting at that table in the cafeteria on that fateful day, that we would become so close, closer than friends, closer than sisters even. Then again, I doubt I would've ever imagined the life I ended up leading.

Amy played percussion in the school band when we met. However, the school band became pretty dull for her, and chorus class got bland for me before the end of the first semester. Because of this, it wasn't long before we decided to drop the school programs for something of our own. We wanted to start a band and we did.

<hr>

"And a one, two, three, four!" Amy shouted, slamming on her cymbals with the force of a hundred men, and I met her force on my keyboard, playing trills and glissandos and just coming down on the keys like a tyrant. Pyrotechnics went off around us as the laser show hit its peak. We crashed to the ending and that's when the thunderous applause came over us.

In the audience, my mom smiled, clapping politely. Amy's mom stood next to her, whistling and stomping and clapping. I looked around and the fantastical vision faded. No, we weren't in Wembley Stadium. We were in North Carolina, a long way from England. This was the Forest Hills Middle School yearly talent show and, based on the faces of the judges, we weren't going to win. Their straight-mouthed smiles seemed to indicate that our passion outweighed our talent by a few years. As they started to scribble a few short notes on their score sheets, I stood from my keyboard and bowed before following Amy off the stage.

"That was amazing! We killed it! Do you think we won?"

she asked, almost bouncing off the walls as we walked to the bathroom.

I remembered the faces of the judges, but shrugged it off. "I think it's anyone's game, but I think we did well." *We did okay, but we could do* better. *We needed about six more months of practice and we would've dominated. Can't crush Amy's hopes, though. Not yet.* I looked in the mirror and adjusted the bow clip that I had in my hair. It had slid through my blond side bangs a bit during the performance. I sighed. Why couldn't I look cool like Stevie Nicks?

"I think they liked it. It's our best song yet. There's no way we didn't win."

Amy was just as much of a dreamer as I was. As we sat in the audience and watched the other acts, we talked about what we would do with the prize money, a whole $50.

"We could use it to buy new cymbals," she suggested, gesturing to her pink kiddie drums that still sat on the stage, just out of the way of the other acts.

I looked at how dully they shone and recalled how tinny they sounded. "Yeah." My keyboard was stranded on stage, stuck behind a kid failing at performing a magic trick. It was a heavy hunk of junk that was over thirty years old. Some of the preprogrammed sounds had stopped working years ago, instead replaced with a single dull tone that would play regardless of which key was pressed. "Or we could use it to buy a new keyboard."

Amy nodded, thoughtfully, before her face lit up. "I have a great idea."

"What?"

"We could buy a banner with our band name on it! It's exactly what we'll need for all the shows we're going to play!"

I nodded in unison with her. "I think you might be onto something here, Amy."

Unsurprisingly, we did not win that talent show or purchase a banner, not that $50 would've been enough to really accomplish much of anything. But, the drive that came out of wanting to win sparked the creation of a whole new band once we met Tom in high school. We all had the same English class together. Amy and I learned through the teacher's dreadful ice breaker games about Tom.

"Okay," Ms. Miller said, "we're going to go around the room and introduce ourselves. Go ahead and tell us your name and two interesting facts about yourself. Let's start over here." She pointed at the first row and a girl spoke. I fidgeted in my seat, situated in the second row. *This is so annoying.* I looked around the room and caught Amy's eye. The teacher had arranged the seats in alphabetical order, so for once we were separated. Amy grinned at me from her spot at the end of the first row. I rolled my eyes and grinned back. I knew exactly what she was going to say. *"My name is Phil Collins. I play drums and I'm bald."* I chuckled to myself as we inched closer to Amy's turn. *Here we go again.*

"'Sup. My name is Phil Collins. I play the drums and I'm a bald British dude." The class filled with awkward chuckles, about a generation too late to know who Phil Collins was, but just the right age to know it was a dumb joke.

"Students, please. Now, Miss Collins. Care to try that again?" Ms. Miller said, clearly unimpressed.

Amy grinned, "Fine. I'm Amy Collins. I play the drums and I am not a bald British guy."

Classic Amy.

The class went on and soon it was my turn. The jitters that had plagued me as I waited vanished the second I was called. "My name is Sam Roland, but Amy calls me Stevie Ray Vaughan, and I'm a singer and keyboardist."

"How sweet. I hope that you all make lots of friends in this class like Amy and Sam have," Ms. Miller said. *Yeah, it won't seem so sweet when Amy and I take over this class with our nonsense.*

After that, I zoned out. I would really meet these people in group work or lunch or something. This time was for zoning out and thinking of our music. And, of course, to think of my crush—Michael Andrews—who was in my science class. Some time passed and then my ears pricked up. *A guitarist?*

"Oh wow, Tommy! When did you start playing the guitar?" Ms. Miller asked.

"I started taking lessons when I was six. Played ever since." His answers were short and to the point. No frills.

I whipped around and looked at Amy, who nodded back at me. We needed this guy for our band.

When the bell rang, I immediately went up to him, "Hey. Your name is Tommy, right?" He looked at me through his long blond hair, which was only slightly longer than my own.

"Tom, but yes. You're Samantha?"

Amy walked up and joined us.

"I'm Sam and this is Amy."

"Nice to meet you guys." He said, standing up and adjusting his gray Led Zeppelin shirt before packing his backpack.

"So, we were wondering—"

"Would you like to join our band?" Amy blurted out, cutting me off. Tom looked up. "It's called Playground," she elaborated and I grimaced.

"It's an older name. We're thinking of changing it. You know, rebranding a bit," I added, hoping we didn't scare him off with our band name from middle school.

His hazel eyes seemed to scan the contents of his backpack as he thought, but he eventually gave a single nod. "Yeah, sure."

Tom has always been the quiet one of the group. We found out later that he thought we were coming up to flirt with him and he was so glad that we weren't that he immediately joined the band out of pure relief. No wonder we used to call him Nervous Nellie.

———

It took us a little bit longer to find a bass player, but he was worth the wait. When it comes to stereotypes, no one defies them as hard as David. Where most bass players are quiet, stoic, and reserved, he is very much not. We met David through Tom in eleventh grade.

"How have you been hiding a bass player from us this entire time!" Amy yelled.

"Yeah! We only mention that we need one every two days! And you just now mention this guy to us?" I added. Tom looked at us from across the lunch table. The cafeteria was the bustling epicenter of Johnson High School, being that there was no auditorium, and today was no different with the new revelation.

"I wasn't hiding him." Tom took a bite of his square shaped pizza. "I just forgot."

"How do you forget that?" Amy exclaimed, nearly crushing her apple in her hand.

"When can we meet him?" I asked. Tom shrugged in response before squinting at something in the distance.

"Looks like right now."

A guy with shaggy black hair with white streaks walked up to the table. "Hey Tom! Hey girls! Nice to meet you! My name is David!" He exuded a radiant sunshine that directly conflicted with his black clothing, silver chains, and dark eyeliner.

Amy lit up immediately, "Hey! Do you want to join our band?"

"Sure!"

David has always been a bit of a golden retriever, despite his dark aesthetic.

"We need a new name."

The sounds of the cafeteria seemed to swirl around us, fixing us as the center of a cacophonous hurricane of chatter.

"What, you don't want to be forty going by Playground?" I asked, wiggling my eyebrows at Amy.

"I just feel like they might not let us near a playground at that point," she replied, and Tom choked on his milk.

"I'm just saying."

"I don't know," David started. "I like Playground. I think it shows we're playful." He took a bite of his pizza. "Light and fun."

"I'll take your advice when you learn some basic table manners, you dorkus," I said, shoving a napkin in his face.

"As fun as we are, I feel like we are more than that. Deeper. More level," Amy said.

"And we've got two girls. We should mention that somehow," Tom said, finally seeming to collect himself post-milk suffocation.

"Well, it's not a big deal that we're girls. We can be rock stars too. We're not special for that," I said, crossing my arms.

"No, but we can market that to our advantage. We aren't special, but we are different—at least in this industry. It'll help us stand out some," Amy said.

"Okay, so what are some girl words?" I asked and glanced around. Lunch was still in full swing, but the bell would ring soon. My eyes flitted over the club posters on the walls. Geek

Club, Music Club, and Math Club were of no use to me. But then I saw it.

"Graceful Gals Dance Club."

"Huh?" David asked.

"Graceful is a girl word. Maybe we could play with that."

"What are we? A church band?" David shook his head.

"No, but we're respectable. 'Grace' shows that," Amy replied.

I tossed the word around in my mouth, thinking.

Tom spoke up. "Well, we're respectable, but not a ton." A smile pulled at his mouth.

"We're coming up on it? On the way to? Working on?" David rattled off.

"Approaching."

The bell rang. Lunch was over, but we stayed still. Amy repeated herself. "Approaching Grace." We looked at each other for a moment before we each started nodding, first slowly and then vigorously, smiling and laughing.

Approaching Grace was born.

With the addition of David, our lineup was complete. It was during this time in high school that we would really nail down what we wanted to do as a band. A band of dreamers, we aimed for Neptune and beyond. And we weren't about to fall short. It was time to get to work.

Start Me Up

THE BAR WAS RATHER quiet that night. The bartenders were clearly paying no attention to us as we put the finishing touches on our sound system and equipment before taking the stage.

"Hey guys, I still can't hear anything from my monitor," Amy said.

"We'll fix it in a minute. Can everyone else hear?" I asked. We had been working for hours already, setting up the equipment and getting situated in the room. As we worked, a small crowd entered the room, settling in at the bar that framed the venue. Now, a subtle buzz of vague interest and slight excitement grew around us as everyone wondered what was in store.

"Yeah, I'm ready. Let's go!" David exclaimed. I looked at Tom, who nodded in agreement.

"All right." I gestured for everyone to go stand in the middle of the stage. We got in a circle and I started my nightly sermon. "Listen up, guys. Let's make it something great tonight. If we can keep their attention or, God willing, draw a crowd, we can probably get back in here next month." Tom was the first to nod, then Amy, and lastly David's shag joined in. I gave a single nod in response. "Okay. Let's do it."

I walked to my keyboard at the front of the stage and checked that the settings were all right for the first song. I made eye contact with Tom and he started the song, a cover of "Baptism By Fire" by Stadium. Amy, Tom, and I kicked in with the a cappella opening, causing some of the patrons to turn away from the bar and look at us. Encouraged by this slight show of interest, I took my eyes off of the keys and made eye contact with the crowd. As soon as I started this campaign, I flubbed the introductory piano part, making the man I was ogling turn back to his drink. *Come on, Roland. You've been playing these songs for two years. Don't mess up the material you conquered at seventeen. Focus.*

The song hit its climax and the harmony kicked back in. I heard Amy overshoot her note, landing on a higher pitch than intended. It was at that moment that I remembered: we hadn't set up her monitor, which meant she was flying blind—or rather, deaf—for the duration of the set. *Shit.*

We finally staggered to the end of the song, giving it a pathetic *thump* of conclusion on the drums. The measly crowd offered a few claps and I sighed as Tom went ahead and started the next song on our setlist. *It's gonna be a long night.*

Despite our many errors on that first night, Johnny's Pub booked us again. And again. And again. And again. We were able to gain a small following of locals who started showing up at all of our shows. It was at Johnny's Pub that we met another bar owner who would be instrumental to breaking us into other bars: Jake.

"Hey guys! Awesome set. Can I talk to you?" he asked as we staggered off stage.

"Well, we only have a fifteen-minute break and I really have to go to the bathroom. Could this wait a minute?" The sweat dripping down my back was the least of my worries as I did a little dance in place. *Hydration is a double-edged sword.*

"Yeah, of course."

I smiled and started towards the bathroom at the back of the room. Jake followed me.

"You know, I think that you guys would be perfect for my bar."

"Oh yeah?" I asked, navigating through the moderately sized crowd.

"Definitely. I could get you guys a Thursday night slot: showcase band. An hour of you guys doing your thing in front of a bunch of other musicians. After the showcase, there will be an open jam led by our house band." I walked past a pool table full of drunk twenty-somethings and just barely escaped becoming a shish kabob.

"Listen, I'll have to talk to the guys and see when they're available." I put my hand on the bathroom door. "Give me your contact information and I can—"

"We're willing to pay you $150. Each." My hand dropped from the door handle. *That's way more than we're being paid by this shithole.*

"All right. I still have to talk to the rest of the band, but I believe we'll be available to do it."

"Perfect. See you this Thursday!" he announced and walked off.

"Wait, *this* Thursday? I don't even know where your bar is!" I yelled after him, but he was gone—lost in the crowd of drunkards and pool players. I sighed. *This better be worth that $150.* I grabbed the bathroom door handle once more to go in just as Amy walked out.

"Hey, are you ready? Our break is over. It's time to go back," she said. I groaned loudly and turned away, resigning myself to holding it for one more hour. We navigated back through the small crowd. "What was that guy talking to you about?" she asked.

"He might be our way out of this place." Amy smiled at me and I couldn't help but smile back. "We're moving up, baby!"

Jake's bar ended up being a place called Shots in the nearby town of Lifeson. Being that Lifeson is just outside of Graham County, the last dry county in North Carolina, the bars there end up getting a lot of traffic. As promised, Jake got us a Thursday night gig, and while we didn't know what to expect, we knew it wasn't this.

Cigarette smoke billowed out into the cold night air as Tom pulled open the door to the bar, and I cleared my throat out of habit. "Well, this is less than ideal."

Amy gave me a quick pat on the shoulder before quickly dipping into the fog to investigate. The stage was small, but still bigger than the one at Johnny's Pub and the seating area was quite large, reflective of the usual crowd size.

"Look at the drum riser!" Amy ran to the stage and pointed, excitedly. The stage was topped with a smaller stage for the drums, inlaid with glitter so that the platform shone in the stage lights. A smile tugged at my lips and I left her and the boys to check out the stage while I searched for Jake. I didn't have to look far.

"Ah, Sam!" Jake called me. "So great to see you! And you got here on time. That's perfect."

"I guess you don't see that a lot," I said with a hint of a question in my voice.

"Oh, well you know musicians. Usually at least one guy is late."

"Well, my band runs a tight ship. We always try to show up together and on time, if not a bit early."

"Sounds like we should get on swell, then," Jake said with a smile. "Now, follow me. I'll show you some of the electrical stuff. It's a bit sticky back there, to be honest with you. Nothing bad has happened yet, but it's better to be safe than sorry." I nodded and followed him back to the stage where the band had already started setting up their equipment.

(Oh, if Jake only knew.)

We exceeded our own expectations, which is always a nice surprise. The crowd, which had to have been upwards of eighty people, responded to us enthusiastically, dancing and singing along to our short set. After we were done and the jam had started, both Tom and Amy got pulled up several times during the night to play with the other musicians. As for David and I, we were busy making connections and talking to people.

After a few hours of this, things wound down and we got the go-ahead to pack up our instruments. As Amy helped me with my keyboard, Jake walked up to us.

"You guys did pretty good tonight."

"Thank you, sir," David said with his trademark dimpled smile.

"You are welcome. Anyways, here is your money and a deal." He handed us a check and I scrunched up my eyebrows. A deal? "I want to have you guys in here again as soon as possible. What do you think of doing a once-a-month deal?" I looked at the band and silently asked them their thoughts. With a nod from each of them in hand, I turned to Jake.

"That would work very well for us. Thank you."

"Of course. Now, I want you guys in here on the last Saturday of every month. Typical, full four-hour show. Deal?" We nodded and Jake shook our hands. "I'll see you in a month, kids," he said, and then left for his office in the back. I closed the zipper on my keyboard bag and took it to our minivan.

Shutting the door, I heard Tom behind me say, "I think this might actually work."

"This could change our lives," David responded, sounding as though the wind had been knocked out of him.

"It's just another gig, guys. Don't be so serious. It's not life or death here. I'm waiting for us to get big, like *big* big," Amy added.

"This is how we get big, Amy. Steps of a ladder," David said.

David didn't realize yet exactly how right he was about this, it would change our lives, specifically mine. And Amy was wrong about the "life or death" thing, as we would later discover.

The Electric Mayhem

IN MANY WAYS, Shots became like our second home. Sure, we played at other bars, but Shots was one of the few constants at this point in time. Our coveted Saturday night gig helped us build our fan base more than any place had before and we were now able to say that we were popular in several counties. Yes, Shots had changed our lives, but it didn't stop at just growing a fanbase. No, my life was forever changed at Shots one November night.

"Sam, where can I find a power cable?" Tom shouted from across the room.

I pulled my head out from behind the drums where I was running wires. "What kind of power? Instrument or normal?"

"Normal."

"Look in the blue tote with the gray lid. It should be labeled 'electrical.'"

"Got it," he said, pulling a cable out of the tote.

"You're welcome," I responded before getting out from

behind the now-ready and -mic'd drums. *The drums are done. Just a million more things to go.*

***

The crowd that night was decently sized, not our biggest there, but definitely not our smallest. They had a great energy, though, and it was pretty fun overall. I would be lying if I said that I wasn't very excited about my new stage outfit. We had been working so frequently that we had made enough money for some more frivolous expenses. As I moved and danced during the show, the lights reflected nicely off of my new red corset-style top and white pleather pants.

At this point in time, our sets were about sixty-percent covers and forty-percent original songs, which we were proud of. Not many bands were doing that so it helped us stand out, and people seemed to enjoy the new tunes.

As our song "New Start" began, I started jumping up and down, hyping up the crowd.

"All right everyone, I know you've heard us do this one before. Sing along and dance, I know you want to!" The crowd was responding great, following my jumping and cheering. Amy hit the crash cymbal, indicating my cue and as I opened my mouth to sing, I noticed something.

"Hey, hey. Break it up," I said.

The crowd turned away from the stage and towards the fight. It started small, but it was contagious, spreading like wildfire. *Shit.* I turned to Tom and David. "Quick, pull the equipment back." We dragged the speakers off the edge of the stage and I grabbed my keyboard as we worked to pull everything towards the drum set.

"Let's get out of here," Amy said, taking the charge to lead us out of the front door.

As the fight raged on inside, David paced in the alley

beside the venue. "Guys, what do we do? All our stuff is in there! What if someone takes something?"

"I doubt anyone is worried about our equipment when they're trying to dodge fists," Tom said, leaning up against the wall.

"That's the perfect time to steal something! Or something could get broken. I just bought a new bass and—"

"David, don't worry. We'll be back in there soon."

"How do you know that, Sam?" The side door of the building opened up, revealing Jake with a sour expression.

"Sam, can I talk to you?"

Oh great.

I stepped through the door and into the office, closing the door on my friends. The silence in the room was stifling, but I wasn't going to break it, fearing the horror of saying the wrong words. The sound of the fight in the other room was gone, indicating that it was finished as quickly as it had started. Jake slouched in his desk chair, letting the overly plush pleather absorb him. He dropped his hand from his face and looked at me, though he didn't meet my eyes.

"You're fired."

"Are you kidding?" Of all the things he could've said, I wasn't expecting that.

"Did you see that fight out there? We can't be doing that." Neon lights from the beer signs on his office walls reflected off of his face, highlighting lines and bags that I hadn't noticed before.

I held my ground. "We didn't start the fight. We were playing and everyone was having a good time until some idiots started it up. We were just doing our jobs."

"It doesn't matter. We can't risk it."

I threw my hands up in the air, though Jake still wouldn't actually look at me. "Just ban the guys who were fighting. We weren't involved."

"We did ban them and now we're firing you. I'm sorry, Sam."

The rage in me reached a boiling point. "Yeah, you'll be sorry, Jake. Your patrons love us and when you lose them, you'll be sorry." I crossed my arms. *Take that, asshole.*

"These guys see every show here. They come for the cheap beer and the waitresses' tits. They don't care what's playing in the background."

I had the door handle in my hand before he finished his sentence. "We'll see about that." I slammed the door behind me as I entered the alley, making the guys jump out of their skin.

"What was that about?" David asked.

"Sam?" Amy called, but I was already headed for the front door to get back to the stage.

"Come on. We have to break down the stuff. We're fired." We entered through the front and I went straight for the stage. We were all silent except for David's incessant, unanswered questions. The kettle was screaming and I just couldn't deal with him right now.

I started pulling the gear off the stage as they watched me, carelessly grabbing and pulling things. I finally grabbed hold of the main power plug, gently tucking my pointer finger in between the prongs to get a grip on it before pulling. But in setting my grip, I felt the strangest sensation. It was over-whelming, but I couldn't get away from it. To the outside world, it wasn't exactly clear what was going on, but it felt like all the lights were being turned off and on in my head. Eventually, the lights turned off and stayed off for a while.

I woke up on the stage, flat on my back, with Amy, Tom, and David all looking down at me.

"Oh, thank God, you're alive." The words fell out of David's mouth like a prayer, so smooth and fast that I didn't understand them at first.

"We need to go to the hospital," someone said, voices mixing and blurring into mush.

Those words I understood and shook my head no, feeling my brain rattle in my skull. "M'fine."

"There's scorch marks on your clothes."

"M'fine." More emphasis, more resistance.

"I'll watch her while you two finish breaking down so we can get out of here." Amy's face re-entered my field of vision as the other two faded out. "If you die on me, I'll kill you." My chuckle was joined by hers, but I had to stop because it hurt too much to laugh. As I laid there, my vision cleared up, and by the time we left, I could finally think again. Amy helped me out of the venue and into the van.

"Hey. Did we get paid?" I asked.

"He wasn't going to, but then you fried yourself, so we got standard rate."

"Hhmph." I settled into the passenger seat. "Well, you're welcome, I guess." She closed the door and got in the driver's seat. Homebound at last.

Amy carried me into our house, leaving Tom and David to look on in shock at her strength.

"Amy, you don't have to carry me. My legs work."

"Shut up. You just got electrocuted to kingdom come and won't go to the hospital, so I'm not going to let you just walk around like you didn't just almost die." She tossed me onto the burgundy couch that decorated our living room. I landed with a huff and sat up on my elbows.

"I didn't 'just almost die.' I just got a little shocked. I'm perfectly fine, Amy."

She tugged at her brown hair fervently. "There are *scorch marks* on your *pants*!"

"It's because they're pleather! It's plastic!"

Amy threw her arms down and then threw herself into an adjacent chair. As the dust settled, David and Tom eased into the scene, settling into the ugly brown couch next to the chair. Three sets of eyes shot towards me as I sat up all the way and swung my legs onto the floor.

"I'm going to take a shower."

Amy's flippant arm wave showed that she didn't care, but her soft eyes betrayed her. I stood up slowly, feeling my feet steadily under me. Pleased, I smiled.

"See. I told you." I started towards the stairs. "But, I'll keep the bathroom door unlocked anyway." The tension in the room began to dissipate and I nodded to myself. *Always so nervous.*

In the bathroom, I evaluated of myself. I looked like hell. As if in a cartoon, my hair was messed up. Not exactly standing straight out, but clearly ruffled quite a bit. And my clothes had black marks on them like Amy had said. The most disturbing part was my left hand, which now had a decently sized black burn on it. I hesitated for a moment, looking at it, but then took a breath in. *I'll just look up how to care for this online. It'll be fine.* I started the water for my shower and began to undress, checking the rest of my body for burn marks. Having given myself a good once over and found nothing, I got into the shower.

Under the water, I continued to study my burnt hand. It was pretty numb, but I could feel the nerves start to come alive as the streams hit the skin. Luckily, the burn only covered the bit that was touching the plug when I grabbed it. Or at least that's what it looked like. My eyes traveled down from the injury to my forearm. My tattoo, only a few months old, survived the incident unscathed. I ran my fingers over the words and read them aloud. "Light me up and burn me down, can't stop me from coming back around." They were lyrics from my favorite Stadium song, "Keep Coming Back." Closing my eyes for a moment, I nodded, the words of the tattoo seeming more literal now than originally intended. I laughed, but quickly opened my eyes as I felt myself swaying. I grabbed onto the walls and waited for my heart to return to its normal rhythm. *Yeah, I'm gonna have to Google these symptoms.*

Looking back at it all...yeah, I should've gone to the hospital. But hey, I was young and stupid and you make mistakes like that sometimes. That being said, I don't advise that you do what I did when I was younger. If you can, go to the hospital when you're injured, or at least go to a doctor of some sort. Just because I got some cool tricks (which you'll learn about shortly) doesn't mean that it will happen to you in the same circumstances. Take care of yourself, people. Or I might be seeing you on the other side....

Who You Gonna Call?

The time after the accident is somewhat hazy to me. I remember that I had a hard time sleeping and felt really uncomfortable in my body, but the other details seem to escape me now. Despite my injuries, we were still working. Working and planning for the future.

"I want to go on tour."

"Tour? Sam, you're still recovering from your little electrical mishap, remember? Do you really think we should be touring right now?" Amy said.

I sat up on the couch, getting out of my reclined position of contemplation, and shook the ghosting feeling of the electrical charge from my limbs. "If not now, then when? Besides —just a little one. Let's cover the state and then we can go from there."

Amy nodded, her lips pursed. "Okay. Tell me your plan."

"My plan?"

"Oh, don't pretend you brought this up without preparing an overly elaborate plan first."

I smiled. "We travel from east to west, of course. We hit every major town. We'll take our van. There's plenty of space for us to sleep in the back if needed—"

"We *did* take out the back seats for this particular reason."

"This tour will expand people's knowledge of us. Sure, we're known in a few counties, but we need to be bigger and this will help. Plus, we can get a ton of content out of it for our social medias. We can have our friends take photos of us at different places. *And* it'll get us tighter as a band. We'll have to figure out gas money and living situations, but if we sit down and budget it out beforehand, I think we can handle it."

Amy listened to my rambling with a smile. "Sam, you're vibrating. You've really been thinking about this for a while, haven't you?"

"Haven't we all?" I looked at my healing hand. There would certainly be a scar there for the rest of my life, a reminder of that night. "Jake firing us was a catalyst. That's when I decided we had to do it. It's our time to branch out." I grabbed Amy's hands, wincing, but holding her tight. "Do you agree with me, Phil? Am I right on this?"

Amy nodded, a veil of brown hair falling into her face, but she still looked me in the eyes. "You know I'd follow you to hell and back, Stevie Ray."

I pulled her into a tight hug and then got up. "Let's go tell the boys."

"I knew saving my vacation and sick days would pay off," David said, throwing his clothes into a suitcase.

"I'm sure you could've just quit and come back after the

tour. It's just a coffeehouse." Tom folded his shirts and placed them in his own suitcase.

"A coffeehouse with a drink named after me!"

"Boys, stop tiffing. You can save that for the van tonight," I said.

"A month in a van with these two. How did we think this would be a good idea?"

I laughed at Amy as I clicked my new hardcover keyboard case closed.

"I still can't believe we're doing this," she said, rolling her suitcase into the small foyer of our shared house.

"It *is* pretty surreal. But, I know what I'm doing and, looking at all the numbers, we're set. This is our time, Ams. Now help me put my keyboard in the van."

That night we drove out east to Wilmington. After making tons of phone calls and talking to damn near every bar in the state, I had booked us twenty shows in thirty days. Our first show was the next afternoon—a happy hour slot at Krazy Kyle's. But, for the night, our goal was to reach the motel where we'd be staying for the next few nights. As Amy drove into the night, I held my notebook and calendar out in front of me, steadied in a ray of moonlight, and nodded to myself. *This is going to work. It's actually going to work.*

Once we got to the motel in Jacksonville, we started to unpack the gear as Tom went in to get the room key.

"Remember, anything you don't want stolen comes inside," Amy said.

The room was very plain, with beige walls, a small TV, and a printed painting of a vase of flowers situated in the wall space between the two beds. To make it clear: this place was tiny. The two beds were squeezed in so tight they touched the walls, but we didn't choose it for its beauty or space, so it would do. I nodded my head, the room having been properly assessed, and set down my two bags before rolling my keyboard into the room. Collapsing on the bed, I sighed.

"I'm claiming this bed for me and Amy."

"Oh come on," David complained, pulling a fit of childish jealousy.

And with my shoes still on, I fell asleep on top of the bed.

On the third day, we all decided that Tom and I should go shopping for groceries.

"We can't have David go shopping or we'd be left with only Sour Patch Kids and those soft cookies to eat for the rest of week," Amy had reasoned. With Amy's point in mind, Tom and I set out in the van.

As Tom drove, I stared out the window, taking in all the sights. "There're a lot of people out today. Must all be going to the beach."

"Maybe. Doesn't really look like a lot of people to me."

"That's because you're drivin'. Look when we get to the light. It's a busy day." People were everywhere. People in bathing suits, people with beach chairs, people with picnic baskets. People, people, people. The light went red and Tom brought the van to a stop. I watched his hazel eyes scan the sidewalks, taking special care to look at both sides twice.

"There's like ten people out, Sam. We been livin' in the country too long?" The light turned green and I felt my face twist up. *Hmm. Maybe it's from the shock. Mild hallucinations.* I tried to shake it off, but it didn't leave me until the cool metal of the shopping cart brought me back to reality. Tom piled frozen dinners, canned goods, and fruit into the cart as I pushed through the store.

"Hey, do you think we can get some—oh!" The cart

screeched to a halt as I avoided hitting someone in front of me in the aisle. Just a moment before, the aisle had been empty besides Tom and I, but now this older lady stood right in front of my cart. Before I could say anything, she looked at me with a startled expression and then disappeared, right into thin air.

"What was that, Sam?" Tom called.

I gestured at the space in front of me, but my words didn't cooperate. Finally, I looked back to Tom. "I was going to ask if we could get some frozen chicken nuggets."

"Yeah, sure. Though, you don't have to ask that. We're all adults." Tom spun around and continued to walk down the aisle. "Except David, of course."

For the rest of our grocery trip, I tried to blink away the people in the store, watching as Tom did not react to them as I did. *I'm gonna need some meds for this.* He led me to the checkout and then we were on our way back to the motel, with questions left unanswered.

As the freezer food cooked in the microwave, we rifled through our suitcases for stage clothes.

"So, we'll go set up, play the show, get paid, break down, and come back here," I said. The group around me nodded. "John will be there at five to take photos and videos after we start. Remember, this is a debut, so act, play, and dress to impress."

"Okay, Mom," David said, and I smiled,

"If I didn't love you, I'd kill you one day."

"Yeah, but you *do* love me, so I'm safe."

"For now. Now, let's get the stuff in the van."

The days of the tour seemed to fly by like nothing. We were playing every day and the hours and days themselves seemed to be getting a little foggy. But, we stayed on top of things like a military unit. We had the process set like clockwork and at three o'clock on the dot, we rolled our gear onto the back patio of our next gig at The Tiki Spot, a bar and grill on Wrightsville Beach.

"We have two hours before showtime, so let's get to work." Amy set about putting her drums up while the rest of us started wiring into the house sound system.

"Do you really think you should be dealing with the electrical there, Sam?" David asked, looking up from the wall socket.

"People who've been electrocuted are more likely to get shocked again," Tom said, and I dropped the cables in my hands.

"Less work for me, then. Thanks for all the research, guys." I huffed off and headed back to the stage. *I'll just set up my keys then.* As I went to grab my case, I noticed a man walking towards us. He had longish gray hair and a face that betrayed his years of experience in bars.

"You guys Approaching Grace?"

"We're trying to." I extended my hand. "Sam Roland, lead singer and manager."

"Tony Greuse, owner. We talked on the phone."

"Ah yes, nice to meet you. As you can see, we're getting ready for the show this evening."

He ran his hand through his hair thoughtfully. "Perfect, perfect. Wanted to thank you guys for helpin' us tonight. That other band bailed on us and everyone else was already booked, so we were in a tight spot."

"No worries. Thank you for accepting us."

"Hey Sam," Amy called. "Can you help me out over here?"

"Sorry, got to go. Thank you again, Mr. Greuse."

"We'll talk later," he said, and then disappeared back into the main body of the restaurant.

I went back to Amy. "Hey, you good?"

That's what I was going to ask you. Who was that old guy?" She tightened the wingnut on the ride cymbal.

"He's the owner, but thank you for the rescue call."

"I try my best," she said with a sly smile. I shook my head, smiling, and went to set up my keyboard.

The show was upon us before we knew it and the crowd seemed almost as anxious as we were. While we fretted about putting on a good performance, the audience buzzed about our potential. Would they be entertained? Would they regret not bringing their ear plugs from home? What kind of music would we play? Were we any good at all? The chatter surrounding us was not *all* about us, but it felt like it could be, making me even more nervous.

"This place is serious about happy hour," David said. The sound of clinking glasses, fizzing soda guns, and glass bottles hitting the wooden bar combated with the voices of the crowd for dominance.

"Well, we *are* at the beach," Amy replied.

"Is everybody ready?" I asked.

As the band broke down the equipment, I grabbed our tip bucket. *They must've liked us.* I counted out the money and called out to the guys, "Come on, kitties. Time for supper." An even $23 for each of us, on top of the cool $400 we were being paid from Mr. Greuse.

"Not bad," David said.

"Not bad at all," Tom added, correcting David's behavior, and he nodded, reproved.

"I, for one, want to get out of here. I need a shower," Amy said.

"You and us all." I started moving my gear to our van. "I love outdoor gigs, but if I could be any stickier…"

I got in the van first, sent there by Amy "for my health." David followed me a few minutes later. "Man, if I stay out there any longer, I might pass right out."

I turned up the A/C. "I hear ya. I can't believe there's still so many people out."

David hummed. "Not really. Looks to be only a few stragglers from the show crowd."

I frowned. "Oh." *Again. It's happening again. What is going on? Why is this happening to me? What is wrong with me? How—*

"What?" he asked.

I fiddled with the charms on the dashboard: Amy's graduation tassel, some sea shells, a turtle figurine with a bobbing head, and green fuzzy dice, among other things. *I can tell David.* I sighed and started, slowly, "Since the accident I've been seeing…people who aren't there."

He jumped forward in his seat. "Ghosts?"

My head snapped towards him, "What? No." I shook my head hard. "Visual hallucinations." I settled back in my seat and sighed again. "It's usually people and if this were a movie, I'd definitely call them ghosts, but this is real life." I paused to regain my breath, the words having flown out of my mouth at an uncontrollable rate. "I looked it up. I'm likely just seeing shadows and my electrically fried brain is processing them as people." David was silent in the back seat, a most concerning sign, so I kept going. "Seems like the shock messed me up a bit."

"Oh Sammie—"

I jumped on his words, stomping out his sympathies, "Don't tell Amy. She doesn't know yet."

"Why don't you want her to know?"

We locked eyes in the vanity mirror, briefly, before I dropped my gaze back to the dashboard.

"I don't want her to worry. She's already so worried about me now, so if she knew that I was seeing things? She would send me home." I looked out the window and saw Amy and Tom still wrapping cables and packing up equipment. "We can't go home. We're just getting started," I whispered too quietly for David to hear, holding it soft and gentle like a promise to myself.

"Well, if you ever need help with your ghost problem, I have a Ouija board."

I rolled my eyes. "It's not ghosts, David." I suddenly couldn't decide whether to laugh or cry. *What would that mean for me, if they were ghosts?* "Ghosts aren't real." They *can't* be real.

The driver's side door opened.

"What's all this about ghosts?" Amy asked, getting in the van.

"Nothing. David's just hassling me."

"What else is new?" Tom said, getting in the back beside David.

"Whatever. I call dibs on the first shower," David said.

"No," Amy and I said in unison. She shifted out of park and we were on our way.

Amy rubbed her shoulders as she drove to the motel.

"Tired?"

"Just sore, Stevie Ray." She shook herself out a little bit, keeping her eyes on the road. "But, next time we do this, we should get a bus. It'd be so much easier to fit the drums in an undercarriage instead of..." Her voice faded into the background.

Next time. There's going to be a next time.

Movin' Right Along

As the tour came to a close, I was over the moon. Everywhere we went, we saw warm smiles and dancing asses. It blew our minds that people would actually like us that much.

And of course there were bad nights; there always are. But the good outnumbered the bad. Our social media numbers skyrocketed, reaching highs that I had never even considered possible. So, I began scheming, working, and planning all day and night. Always planning.

Amy held the steering wheel loosely, looking out the windshield with sleepy eyes.

"Falling asleep on me?" I asked from the passenger seat.

"No, not yet."

I looked out at the vast array of stars above. It seemed right for our tour to end in the mountains, to end on a literal high point.

"How do you feel?" I asked.

"About the tour?"

"Yeah."

"I'm glad we're going home." Her grip on the steering wheel tightened.

I slouched. "I am, too."

"No you're not. You could go out every day for a year and still not be satisfied." She smiled a small smile.

"Yeah, you're not wrong. But it's good to go home." I looked at the boys asleep in the back. "I think we all need to rest some."

"Definitely. Speaking of"—she pointed at a rest stop sign —"it's your turn to drive."

I've always liked getting behind the wheel. It helps me think. And as Amy's soft snores filled the cab, I was thinking about what would happen tomorrow when we got back home, when David went back to the coffee shop, when Tom returned to Guitar Center, when Amy went back to being a waitress, and I went back to planning. Planning and thinking. I sighed, adjusting my seat and staring down the road signs. Only a hundred more miles to go. *Planning and thinking. Planning and thinking.*

We got back to our house as the sun came up, the stars having faded away, also returning to their homes. As we pulled into the driveway, I honked the horn. "Wake up. kiddos, we're home." There were groans as I put the van in park and got out, stretching. Tom went and opened the back, moving slowly as he began to pull the gear out and put it on the ground. I grabbed my keyboard from him and rolled it into our old, ragged house. *We're home.*

I looked down at the numbers on the page. *Yes, this'll do.*

"What are you up to, Sam?" Tom asked, sitting down on

the couch, wearing his black Guitar Center uniform. I gestured to the notebook on the table between us.

"I've crunched the numbers and come up with a tour budget, including some funds for a bus!"

"Sam, that's great. We'll be off the ground in no time, then."

"Well, let's not get too crazy. I still have to find an actual bus in our budget. That's the next mountain to climb."

"Do you have any ideas?"

"Yeah, I've found a few lots that specialize in used party buses and RVs and stuff so, we could at least find something to convert into a tour bus."

Tom nodded. "You'll find something." He stood up. "I have to go to work."

"So do I."

"See you later."

"Yeah." I grabbed my car keys and headed to the first lot.

The first lot was a bust. After three hours of having the slimiest man pitch shitty deals to me, I decided I had had enough. And none of the options were going to work. There were missing interior and exterior doors, collapsed bunk beds, missing kitchen appliances, oil eaters, hard starters, and these were the "high line" ones. I had better luck at the second place.

The tour bus in front of us was dull gray with dark windows. The gray paint did a poor job of covering the obvious damage the bus has seen. *Hell, one side of the damn thing looks like a crushed Coke can that got pulled back into shape.* There clearly used to be a logo on the same side, but between the wrinkles and the paint, it was impossible to tell what the logo was.

"How much does this one cost?" I asked the large salesman.

"This one is the most affordable on the lot. It's $1,750 a month," he said, and I nodded. *Yeah the band can't afford that, not with the house rent on top of that.*

"What sort of amenities come with it?"

"Well, there are six bunks, four couches, a half bath, an undercarriage storage space, a bike rack, and a small kitchen, in addition to some other things."

I looked at his large hands as he clenched and relaxed his fingers. *He's nervous.* "It sounds pretty nice. Why is it so cheap?"

The smile on the salesman's face slipped a bit, "I'm afraid I don't understand what you're asking.

I ran a hand through my hair indifferently and looked at my notes.

"Well, you just listed off a full set of amenities. I've only seen that on the really high-end buses, which means this was clearly one once. So, either you are telling me a bold-face lie about the contents of this bus or this bus is bad for you. Something either happened to or on this bus that makes the average buyer weary of it." As I went on, I watched the color drain from his round face. "So tell me, what's wrong with the bus?"

The salesman glanced around the lot and saw no one. He crouched down and got so close to me that I could smell his lunch.

"You really want to know, missy? Okay. This bus is over thirty years old. In the eighties, it was used by a cartel to smuggle cocaine over the border and into the living rooms of everyday people." It was now his turn to watch me, but I continued to stand tall. "It's been shot up, beaten up, stripped down, and struck by an eighteen-wheeler. We think it was bought with drug money." My eyes got a bit big when he said that, but he quickly continued, "Now, there's nothing illegal about owning this vehicle, people just don't want it because of its checkered past." The salesman stood up straight again. "So, will you be another driven away by its history?"

I stared at the bus intently, as if trying to see through it with x-ray vision. *With that kind of baggage, I bet I can get him down from $1,750.* I made a show of adjusting my checkbook in my bag to show my continued interest in the vehicle.

"Show me the interior first," I instructed.

The salesman clicked his tongue and hit the button to open the door, then waved me inside.

After an hour, we got off the bus. The sweaty salesman was even sweatier, either nervous or determined. Or simply hot from being in the bus.

"Okay, let's talk business now."

"We weren't before?" he asked, and I smiled. We walked to his office, a room that reeked of the seventies, what with its ugly carpet and mismatched wallpaper. I sat down in one of the crusty-looking chairs as he got behind his desk. "Okay miss. Hit me with your best shot."

I crossed my hands in my lap and looked straight at him with a plain expression. *Just ooze confidence and he will bend. Just ooze it.* "You were offering $1,750 a month to rent the tour bus. That's not a bad deal, however, I think I have an idea that can help both of us out."

The salesman leaned forward, settling on his desk. He straightened out a nameplate that read Larry Stevens before gesturing for me to go on with my offer.

"You've spun me an elaborate story about the history of this bus. It sounds like quite a burden for you." I leaned back in my seat and uncrossed my legs, creating a stance of dominance. "How about I just buy the bus from you? That would take the burden off of your shoulders. You'd never have to worry about that hunk of junk ever again."

He seemed to mull this over in his head, looking as though he was almost trying to savor the taste of my offer. "You make a good point, kid. But just how much are you willing to pay to *alleviate* my burden?"

"Well, you were saying $1,750 a month. I'm willing to put forward $3,000 for you to never have to deal with that scrap of metal ever again."

"$3,000, huh? That's not a lot—"

"You have to consider that me taking this off your hands includes me having to renovate it. It's barely in working condition. I'll have to pay someone else to fix stuff you'd need to do if someone were to ever rent it. So, consider how my offer saves you the money that you'd have to spend on another renter."

Once again, he tossed the offer around in his mouth, chewing it like cud. "I can do $5,000."

"3,500."

"4,500."

"3,750."

"4,000."

"All right kid. I can do $4,000." I stuck out my hand and he shook it firmly. *Thank God for those unused college savings....*

I followed Amy's van into our driveway, parking the new tour bus outside of the house. I hopped out of the driver's seat.

"So what do you think?" I asked.

Amy looked at the vehicle as the sun set around us. "Well, I'll have to get a better look at it once the sun comes back up, but it'll definitely do. We'll have to do some work, I'm sure."

"Oh yeah, the interior needs a lot of work, but I have some money left in the budget that should get us at least part of the way there."

Amy nodded as we walked into the house. David and Tom were still at work, so that left the two of us. "I guess this means that we're serious now."

I looked up from the notebook I just picked up. "I guess so," I said with a smile.

Amy smiled back at me and turned on the TV. She switched the channel to one of the 24/7 rock radio stations. As she did so, "Say My Name" by Stadium came on. "Come on, Stevie Ray. Time for a celebratory dance party!"

I stood up and joined her in front of our small TV. She cranked the volume as we jumped up and down erratically, screaming the words to the song. I grabbed her hands and we spun around, dancing like we used to in middle school. It wasn't until the song was over and done and the next one was on that we finally fell victim to our dizziness and fell on the floor, laughing. I grabbed the remote and turned the volume down to a more normal level. "Ah, Amy. We haven't done that in forever," I said, out of breath.

"We haven't been celebrating enough then." She pulled a strand of hair out of her mouth with a noise, then continued. "We've done so much recently. I don't think it's really been sinking in for us. We've been writing like crazy, our social media has exploded, and we've done our first tour all in just the past few months. It's insane! And we've not had nary a dance party or fancy dinner or cake or nothing!"

I laughed. "You're right. I mean, you guys are always so busy with work and stuff." My gaze dropped from hers.

"Hey now, what's wrong?" She lifted my chin with a finger. "We were just dancing. What went wrong?"

"I just—I don't work. You guys do so much and I just— leech off of you. I don't do anything."

She scooched closer to me and grabbed my hands. "Hey, hey, hey. Stop that. I don't want to hear you say that ever again." Amy stood up and pulled me with her. She opened the front door and pointed at the tour bus in the street. "Does that look like not doing anything? Hmm?" She closed the door and pulled me back into the living room, pointing at all of my notebooks on the table. "Accounting, scheduling, budgeting, strategizing, planning. Look at all of the work you do for the band!"

She let go of me and I fell onto the couch. "Just because you don't get paid for it, doesn't mean you aren't working and it doesn't mean that your work isn't important because, without you, we'd still be playing at rinky-dink little bars that close at eleven." She sat down in the chair across from me. "You are our lifeline, Sam. We need you more than you realize, okay? I don't ever want to hear you try to put yourself down like that again, you hear me?"

I nodded.

She reached over and patted my knee. "Now, you know I don't pull out my inspirational speeches for just anyone, so you better appreciate that."

"Oh well, you know I'm not just anyone, so—" A pillow hit me in the face, cutting me off. "So that's how it's going to be?" I grabbed a pillow and returned the blow. "Your speech gave me just enough inspiration to hit you in the face—ah!"

The night devolved into screams and smacks, but the point was still there. I was an asset, an important member of the team. This was so early on in our career. It would be years before anyone saw me as the face of Approaching Grace or anything else, for that matter. In those days, with our green shag carpet and ugly, patterned couches, we were no one. But the fame that we were looking for was right around the corner. Once we boarded that beat-up old bus that sat in our yard, we would never be the same. We would be someone.

Rockin' Down the Highway

"Okay, guys, head to the bus. Move it."

"Yes, Sargent Roland." David stood at attention, saluting me.

I rolled my eyes. "Just shut up and get on the bus."

We began moving like a flock, carrying our luggage out of the house and to the bus in our driveway.

"Let's go ahead and put the instruments in the undercarriage and split the luggage. If you need it all the time, it goes in the bus. If it's stage clothes or something you aren't going to need all the time, stow it," Amy said, and I nodded. Tom grabbed the other end of my keyboard case and we put it next to the drum cases. I handed him his guitars to put on top of my keys. David came up last and put his bass on top.

Then, when we were done, we stood at the open door of the bus, "Okay: rock, paper, scissors, who's driving?" David said. We extended our fists. "Best out of three."

"Rock, paper, scissors, shoot!"

David ended up being the driver for the night, despite his pleas for a best out of five.

"Listen, at least this is a short night. We're not going out of state yet. It's just Raleigh," I said as we got on the bus after him.

"Yeah. It could be worse," he mumbled. I ruffled his hair and moved past him to the bus proper. Over the course of the past few weeks, we had refurbished the bus, cleaning up the dust and grime. Now it was beautiful, in its own way. The first section, right behind the driver's seat, had two long couches, one on each side with a small table for both. The kitchen was also in this section, with a microwave, a pantry cabinet, and a mini fridge that we had stocked with as much food and water as could possibly be crammed in it. In the next section of the bus were the bunk beds. There were six bunks, three on each side. We decided to use the two bottom bunks as on-bus storage. We had put new mattresses, clean sheets, and new divider curtains in each bunk. Next to the bunks was the bathroom, which was just a toilet, sink, and mirror. The back of the bus was another seating area. The whole perimeter was a long, connected couch, covered with blankets and pillows, making it feel reminiscent of a seventies love den or something, but it was comfy. There was also a TV that we bought and connected to Tom's video game console.

I packed my bus bag into a bottom bunk and walked around. Amy and Tom followed suit, with Tom putting David's bag up too. "A whole month in a bus, baby."

"This should be interesting," Amy said, smirking.

"Yeah, you're telling me. A whole month in a bus with these two idiots." I smiled before sitting down on the left couch in the front with my itinerary. "Okay, so David is driving tonight. We should get to Raleigh in no time, but we should stay on top of it. We'll get to Raleigh tonight, meet up with the local crew and set up, eat dinner, do the show, pack up, shower backstage, and then be back on the bus by one. From there, I'll take over driving. In the morning, we'll go to a rest area and switch off. Sound good?"

They nodded.

"Did you hear me, David?"

"Not really, but I agree with whatever you said."

I nodded at the other two with a smile. "Get comfortable, kids. This is home now."

"Where did you say we were playing again?" Tom asked.

"Well, I didn't actually say. I didn't want to freak anyone out, but I realize that this plan could totally backfire, so I'll tell you now. We're going to be the opening band tonight at the Walnut Creek Amphitheater."

"Are you kidding me?!" David yelled from up front.

"*Now* you can hear me?"

"*Now* it's important! Are you kidding?"

"Not at all. Start thinking about what you want to wear. I'm going to start arranging the set list. Send any song suggestions to the editor."

"Oh, I tons of ideas," Tom said, and I patted on the couch next to me,

"Come on then. Let's throw some shit at the wall." He smiled and I opened my laptop.

David pulled the rinky-dink bus into the back of the venue, following the signs that security had alerted him to. I felt the hair stand up on my arms as we passed the crew and band buses for the other two acts on tonight's bill. Whether or not the other guys were nervous, I did not know, but the silence that fell over us was noticeable either way.

"So, what do we do when we get off the bus?" Tom asked, breaking the silence.

I blinked a few times in response. *Good question.* "Honestly, I'm not sure. I assume that we'll run into somebody who we can ask, but I'm flying blind right now."

Tom hesitated and then nodded in response.

Slowly but surely, David pulled the bus into a parking spot, directed by a member of the venue security. As we all stood, we were interrupted by a knock at the door. "David, who is that?" Amy asked.

"I have no idea." He grabbed the handle to pull the door open, letting the intruder into the bus.

"There had to be a safer way to do it than that," Tom muttered.

Onto the bus walked a short, balding man in a black polo shirt, emblazoned with the Walnut Creek Amphitheater logo. When he reached the top of our short stairs, he looked at David. "You don't have the license to drive this thing, do you?"

David sputtered out, "You need a specific license for this?"

I slammed my hand into my forehead, causing the man to turn and look back at us. His serious face pulled into a large smile. "I'm just messing with you kids. Though you should actually get a license or hire someone to do it for you before you get pulled." He watched as the fear rolled off of us and stepped forward, offering a hand to David and then the rest of us., "My name is Reggie, but you can call me Reg. I work for the venue and I'm here to show y'all around."

I looked at Tom and gestured to Reg as if I knew this was going to happen, and then said, "Lead the way."

Reg told us to off-load our equipment and clothes, which were then handed off to his team of local crew. We watched as our luggage walked off and I turned to him expectantly, eyebrow quirked.

"They know the venue better than you guys. They'll get it where it needs to be faster and more efficiently." He gestured for us to follow him and we entered the back of the venue. "That's the name of the game here—speed and efficiency.

With that in mind, I'm going to make you faster and more efficient by giving you a little tour. Follow me." He took us down a series of convoluted hallways that finally led to the belly of the backstage: the dressing rooms. We passed several rooms with name placards for our fellow performers before landing at a single room with our name taped to the door. It was set off to the side, in a bit of a corner. "As you can probably tell, this is the room for the opener. However, WCA prides itself on having one of the nicest opener suites in the region." He opened the door and ushered us in. Our clothing cases were already in the room waiting for us. "You have a shower in that corner, as well as a few mirrors, and some couches as you can see. There is also a microwave over there for your use." Our eyes followed his hands as he pointed out the things in the room. "There is one thing that I should say while we are in this part of the building. This isn't an official order or anything, but I can tell you kids are, well, kids. You're new to this, so let me give you an etiquette tip: don't go knocking on the doors of the other bands. They might come visit you—*might*—and that's cool. But, do not go to them. Lots of bands consider this preshow time to be sacred, with wacky rituals and schedules that they absolutely will not deviate from. So, in the interest of not making enemies out of your allies, don't bother them."

I nodded. "That should be easy enough to do. I'm sure we'll have our plates full with getting ready as well."

Reg nodded back. "That you will. While we carried your gear in, we don't know how you set up the stage. So, I'm actually going to take you there now so we can get started with that." He took us out of the room and down the hallway. The hallway opened up at the end and the sounds of people working were clear and obvious. I looked at Amy with reverence and she wore the same face. *We're here.* Reg took us to the right side stage and walked us on. There was so much going on, but in the middle of the stage were our equipment cases.

"I have to leave now—I have other work to do—but if y'all need anything, ask someone in a polo or ask someone to find me. It was nice meeting y'all." With a smile and a wave, Reg was gone and we were left with the roadies in the middle of the stage.

"Now what?" David asked.

"Now, we work," I said, and headed to our pile of equipment.

The show was upon us before we could even blink. We had set up the equipment and then went back to our dressing room to change and warm up. I looked at myself in the mirror. Most wouldn't consider a half up/half down hairstyle to be too rock and roll, but summer in the South was nothing to sneeze at. I nodded at myself and smoothed down my outfit when there was a knock at the door. Tom opened the door, revealing Reg.

"Well kids, now is your time. Come with me," he said and gestured down the hall with the clipboard he held in his hand.

"Oh my God, we're gonna die," David said.

I rolled my eyes. "David, it's the same thing we've been doing for years now, just on a larger scale. It's okay." I patted his back and headed to the door. "Just do your best like you always do. If we do that, we'll have nothing to worry about."

Reg looked at me and smiled. "Let's go."

We followed him down the hallway we had traversed earlier and headed towards the stage. From the side stage, we could hear the mumblings of the crowd, almost like white noise with its persistence and unclear sound. Different members of the crew handed us our instruments. My microphone and keyboard were already on the stage, so I simply rigged up with my inner-ear monitors so that I could hear us playing over the crowd.

"This feels so weird," Amy said as she put her monitors on.

"Yeah, it's so odd to have these things," I replied.

She shook her head. "No, I mean this." She gestured out at the crowd. "I can't believe we're here."

I followed her gaze and watched the crowd for a moment. "I know what you mean." I turned on the monitors and heard the crowd noise even louder, the sound being picked up by the mics on the stage. "It's only up from here," I said, and looked at her before pulling her in a tight hug. "We're doing it."

"As much as I love a nice, sentimental moment, it's time for you to go on," Reg said, and the lights on the stage dimmed, causing the audience to start cheering.

I nodded at him and grabbed my friends. "Let's go."

I'll never forget that first show. It was the first time we ever did a show of just originals. The crowd had not come to see us, we knew that. We were just a small time band, an up-and-comer. Despite this, we did our best to try and win them over and we did. By the end of our set, we had people nodding their heads, dancing in their seats, and generally smiling and having a good time. We played our hearts out. It was over before we knew it. We lined up at the front of the stage and bowed and the audience applauded us. The roar fell over us and we retreated off the stage, full of adrenaline. We collapsed behind the sound engineer booth, out of breath, exhausted, and jittery. I watched as the local crew ran out and broke down our equipment and brought it off stage. They were taking it to the back, where they would help us pack it up and we'd store it back in the bus. But for now, we were stuck to the ground with sweat, absorbed in the high of live performance.

This isn't so bad. My eyes were fixed on the road ahead of us, my hands tight on the steering wheel. I glanced at the GPS. *Only three more hours of driving to go and then Amy takes over.* I turned up the radio a bit, keeping it just quiet enough to hopefully not wake the others. *Tonight was a good night. Tomorrow we'll be in Atlanta and we'll have to do it all over again. Set up, get ready, suck up, and roll out.* I looked out at how the moon was set in the sky. It wasn't quite full yet, but the stars surrounded it anyway, as though they were drawn to it. *They stuck together, through thick and thin,* I thought, and then laughed at myself, looking back at the road.

"It's just the moon," I said, but glanced back up at it in the sky.

No, it's not just *the moon.*

I hate to say it, but the second day was not much like the first. For one, there was no Reg. An anonymous man met our bus and directed us to our room. Someone else came by to show us the stage, and yet another came for us when it was time to go on. I know now that this is pretty normal, but for us with our one day of experience, it was a bit off-putting. To be honest with you, I don't remember much about the show that day except for the fact that it didn't go that great. I remember us playing to a crowd of mostly empty chairs. It seems the majority of the audience had decided to wait until after the random opener was done to come into the theater. We finished the night tired and disappointed. It wasn't our first lackluster turnout and it was by no means the last, but it always stings. However, the disappointment of the gig isn't the reason I don't have a good memory of it. No—the real reason has to do with how much more memorable the "after party" (as we now refer to it as) that night was.

I couldn't sleep. The lights were off in the bus, my curtain was closed on my bunk. I wasn't too hot or too cold, but I couldn't sleep. Through the sound dampening of my curtain, I could hear the faint sound of David snoring in the bunk above me and the sound of Amy playing Candy Crush across from me. *I can't believe she's still awake. Is she not exhausted? I know I am.* With a sigh, I opened my curtain and did my best to drop from my second-story bunk to the floor as quietly as possible.

Walking to the front of the bus, I stretched. *Only the second night on the bus and I'm already feeling it.* I placed a hand on the small of my back for a moment as I opened the fridge and grabbed a beer. I cracked it open before plopping down on the couch. From the front, I could hear the radio playing softly as Tom drove.

Outside of the window, I could see a flock of stars. *It's as if they're following us.* I chuckled for a moment and then was hit by a memory. "Little star," I said to myself. It's what my mom used to call me, but looking back at our performance, I wasn't so sure. The hundred or so people in the almost 19,000-seat amphitheater made me wonder if we were trying to go too big, too fast. *Am I making a mistake? What if I'm leading us to failure?* I closed my eyes and fought back the urge to cry. *God, I'm doing this all wrong.*

"Hey, what are you doing up?" Tom asked from the front, his voice muddied by the sound of the radio.

"I can't sleep," I said, my eyes still wired shut. *Definitely can't cry in front of the guys. What would I tell them?*

"Wait—you can hear me?"

"I mean, you sound a bit strange back here, Tom, but I can hear—" I opened my eyes and saw him. "You're not Tom," I said.

In front of me stood a man surrounded by a cloud of smoke. He wore tight leather pants, a loose leopard-print shirt with only three buttons done, and a cowboy hat with matching boots. His brown hair was feathered and teased up to the heavens, seeming to lift the hat off of his head. And just under his hat—a face that looked oddly familiar....

"Well, my name is Tom, but most people call me Blades," the strange man replied.

I brought my fists up in front of me and tried to look intimidating in my old T-shirt and gym shorts. *I don't know how to fight, but he doesn't know that. Look tough, look tough, look—*"Okay, 'Blades'. Why are you on our bus? *How* are you on our bus?" *There's no way someone just snuck in.*

Blades paced around for a moment and I followed him with my fists. "I see. They didn't tell you."

"Who didn't tell me what?"

Blades hopped up and sat on our small countertop. "Well, this isn't *your* bus, really. It's haunted."

I laughed. "Yeah, sure, and I'm the tooth fairy. And exactly how does that explain you being here?"

Now it was his turn to laugh. "I'm dead!"

Interlude: Back to the Library

There was a crisp *clap* sound when Sam closed the novel. She looked up and at the crowd, noting that the silence that had descended upon them while she read had not yet been lifted. In the back of the room still stood the group of four men whom she had learned to find comforting over these many years. She sighed a breath of relief at seeing them there, before she took off her glasses and hung them on her shirt, setting the book back on the table. Looking back at the crowd, she smiled.

"That's all folks. You'll have to read the rest to find out what happens next, though I can tell you one thing: the main character survives at the end." She winked at the crowd and a chuckle reverberated through them, effectively cutting the stiff silence in the room. "Now, I understand that it is time for questions?"

At that, Carla ran back into view, standing at the front of the audience, but decidedly not on the tape outlined "stage."

"Okay everyone. In the interest of time and orderliness, we ask you to stay seated and simply raise your hand if you have a question. We also ask that you limit yourself to one question so that we might get to everyone." Carla nodded at me, indicating the end of her spiel, before stepping off to the side to observe.

"All right. Who wants to start?" Sam asked.

The first tentative hand went up. It belonged to the man she had noticed earlier with the tiny baby. "I hate to ask this, but you expect people to believe that you can really see and talk to ghosts? I mean, this is supposed to be a *nonfiction auto-biography*, I thought, and now you're talking about speaking to dead people? I'm just a bit confused." A few people in the crowd began to murmur, largely seeming to agree with the man.

Sam made eye contact with his daughter, the one who was disturbed by Ronnie and Mark's hollering before, and gave her a knowing glance. *Grown-ups. They just don't under-stand, do they?* She resituated herself in her chair before answering.

"It's branded as a nonfiction autobiography because that is what it is. Scientists have long researched the so-called 'next life' and its connections to us. It's by no means a new concept. The fact of the matter is that people have been claiming to be able to interact with spirits for as long as people have been dying. Whether or not they have been telling the truth is up for debate. And whether or not *you* think I'm telling the truth is up to you, but this is my life. I'm not trying to trick anyone; this isn't a ploy for publicity. I felt that this was a story, both of my life and also of the life and death of the members of Stadium, that should be shared. And I'll stand by that until, well, until *I* die."

The man looked a bit sheepish and I gave him a curt nod and then a soft smile. "Well, I'm sure that answer covered a lot of your questions and that's okay. Let's move on. Who's next?"

The next hand flew up. It belonged to an older woman— though, Sam realized, she was not too much older than herself.

Sam called on her and the woman's voice filled the air, soft and smooth and holding the warmth of age.

"Sam, I have been a fan of yours for years. I've followed you since the debut album days and I've just got one question. It's been so long since Approaching Grace broke up—why did you wait so long to write this book?"

"Great question." The voice came from the back. *Ronnie.* Sam fought back the urge to roll her eyes, but a smile caught her instead.

"That's a good question," she started, relenting to Ronnie's teasing. "Well, you've followed my career; I've been busy!" A wave of laughter rose in the crowd. "I didn't really talk about this in the book, because I wanted to keep the focus on the band, but yeah—I went solo after the breakup and it's kept me very busy. We were busy in Grace, but to go from a four-person group to a single person was just a lot."

Sam turned over the novel in her hands, almost as if she only just then realized the book was finished and real. "I didn't even think of writing this book until about seven years ago, at which point I just started to write some anecdotes down when I was on the bus and over time it just grew into this," she said, holding up the book. "So yeah, it took me a bit to get to it, but I thank you all for waiting and for coming here now for the release. Maybe I'll write about my solo career in a while. If I ever ever quit, that is, which means I probably won't," Sam finished with a smirk. The crowd rumbled in support and amusement.

The next half hour was filled with all grades of questions, from the menial (Why did you stick with the name Approaching Grace?) to the personal (Did you ever sleep with Amy?). The crowd laughed at her jokes and commiserated with her tragedies. All was going well.

When it was time for the final question, Sam was unsurprised when the young, dark-haired girl who snapped her photo earlier raised her hand. Sam called on her and in a sweet voice, the girl asked her question. "I was wondering about the ghosts. Are they still here with you or did you help them pass on at some point?"

The question hit Sam right in the gut, forcing the air out of her lungs. Her head dropped towards her lap and she slammed her eyes shut for a moment before forcing herself to slowly lift her head back to meet the girl's eyes. She took a deep breath and then made herself speak.

"Well, it's funny that you ask that, actually." She looked up at Blades and then to Mark, who gave a single nod to her. To everyone else, it looked as if she were pointing to an empty corner of the room, but to her, she was pointing at her friends. "Right there, in the back, are the ghosts, as you called them. I call them Blades, Ronnie, Mark, and Joey. You can't see them, but they're there. Clear as day, for me. Regarding the second half of your question"—she cleared her throat—"about helping them move on, you can read about that in the book. I can promise you, it is a prominent topic, especially towards the end. Thank you." The girl nodded and smiled at her.

Carla walked back in front of the crowd with her hands clasped in front of her. "All right everyone! That concludes our Q&A session. Ms. Roland has been so kind as to also offer to sign a few things, so if you have anything you want signed, please line up. Please simply hand Ms. Roland your item for her to sign and then move on to the next person."

The people lined up as Carla continued her repetitive speech. People had CDs, shirts, and a few had vinyl and posters. And as promised, the dark-haired girl had gone upstairs to print the photo she had taken of Sam, which she signed with a flourish and a heart.

As quickly as it started, it was over, and Carla was walking Sam out of the main room and into the back where she could exit in private. She thanked Carla for her help today and headed out, hopping in the back of the black car with tinted windows that she used for public events. In her hand, she held the hard copy of the book she'd read from earlier. She knocked it against the glass divider between her and the driver and they were off.

The car ride home was not a quiet one, at least not internally. Her mind was racing. The ghosts were not with her; they seemed to dislike being in moving vehicles after so many years on the tour bus. They would meet her at her home, where she would have to do the next step. She looked at the book in her hands, staring at the photos of Approaching Grace and Stadium. Her fingers grazed the image of her friends. *How can I do this? How am I supposed to give them up?* The car pulled into the driveway of her Florida home. She had moved here shortly after the band broke up, leaving the comfort and safety of North Carolina for the thrill of something new and far away from her disillusioned former bandmates. She stepped out of the car and walked through the front doors.

"Hey Sam, great job at the reading!" Joey called, appearing beside her as she headed towards her kitchen.

"Thanks Joey." She reached into one of the high cabinets and pulled out a bottle of bourbon, pouring herself a tall drink.

"It didn't go that bad, Sammie," Ronnie added.

"No, it went quite well," Sam said, and started towards her living room. She settled into a big leather seat, her favorite, and took a sip. Staring at the fireplace, she opened her mouth and the fire was lit.

Mark appeared beside the fire. "It felt safe to assume, on a chilly day such as this, that you'd like a fire. Though it's still weird to me that you have a fireplace in Florida anyway, but whatever."

Sam smiled and rolled her eyes. She felt Blades' presence before she saw him. He was tucked in beside her on the chair, taking a sip of her drink while drawing shapes on her curled-up legs. She leaned in for a kiss, savoring it in case it was to be their last. *God, why did I have to think of that?*

She cleared her throat when the kiss broke and looked at Mark. "Okay, so you say that I just need to finish reading the book out loud and then you guys will be gone?" She pretended that her voice didn't crack when she asked that.

Mark nodded. "Based on the information I found online, you just need to 'tell our story' and then we're gone."

"Yeah, well, we know how reliable online info is," Joey said, and Sam chuckled. *Pretty Internet literate for a guy who never saw a laptop in his lifetime.*

Feeling Blades' gentle touch, now on her arm, she tensed up. "Okay. We have a long night of reading ahead of us, fellas. Get comfy." She took the glasses off of her shirt and put them on again. She cracked the book open with a shuddering sigh.

"It's okay, Sam," Blades said in a whisper, and then kissed the back of her hand.

She nodded and then cleared her throat. "All right, let's see. Ah yes, next chapter. Only The Good Die Young..."

Only the Good Die Young

"You're dead?" I asked, my voice dropped to a whisper. *Was David right? Can I see ghosts now?*

"Last time I checked, yes." There was a coy smile on his face. "I'm sorry if I scared you. It's just been so long since I've talked to anyone alive and they didn't run away screaming. It's good to talk to someone new."

"That's still an option," I said, and dropped my fists. *No use trying to punch a dead guy.* "Also, someone new? Are there more of you?"

"Of course there are. What, did you think I just happened to die here all by myself?" One by one, more ghostly figures appeared from the dark, surrounded by the same cloudy smoke that followed Blades around. As I looked at the three new figures, my breathing almost came to a stop. Blades smiled. "Can you see them too?"

I nodded in a stiff manner, almost as if I was trying the action out for the first time.

"Let's introduce you then," he said and gestured to the first apparition. "This is Joey Rogers, our drummer. Really an animal." The blond man smiled, showing off a lopsided look that was as threatening as it was charming.

Blades continued on with the next ghost. "This is Ronnie Guilder, the bassist of our group. Thunderous player, you'd think he was Entwistle." The bassist's lips pulled into an indiscernible thin line of either thanks or condemnation.

"Lastly, we have Mark Miller. From what I can tell, he's you."

My heart dropped and I could feel the blood drain from my face. *I'm gonna die tonight.*

"Don't kill the girl, Blades." The last ghost stepped forward, offering a brilliant smile that didn't quite meet his eyes and a hand. "I'm Mark. I'm the front man of this whole shindig, that's what that ditz meant." Then, looking at my apparent apprehension, he dropped his hand. "It's a force of habit. People can't touch us anyway."

My shoulders dropped back into position and I found myself standing a bit straighter. "Can any of you tell me what is going on or have I just gone completely crazy?"

Mark's smile slipped a bit. "Well, as Blades said, we are dead. We died on this very bus and we've been stuck here since." He walked around the bus a bit before sitting down on the couch. "I like what you've done to the place." He tried to pat a pillow, but his hand went straight through it. He sighed before continuing, "Actually, we can leave, but no one can see us. This is the only place that people can see us." He ran a hand through his ink-colored hair and stopped for a moment to play with a streak of indigo. "I promise we won't hurt you. As I said, we can't touch the living, but we have no place else to go and to stay hidden like we have is very draining on us, so you'll just have to deal with us." Mark looked up from the blue strand in his hand and back at his bandmates. "I'm sorry, Samantha."

The whole thing made me feel woozy. It was like everything I had ever thought was now being proven as a lie. Spirits had been a part of my understanding of the world, just like demons and angels. But this was nothing like I expected. They weren't supposed to hang around tour buses, decorated in glitter and leather. They were supposed to be in white robes with halos and angel wings or even dressed up in sheets. Anything but this. Anything but these four men standing in front of me.

I shook myself out of my crisis for a moment and caught a glimpse of the clock on the wall. *3:47 a.m. I have to go to sleep. I need to sleep.* I looked around the room again, seeing how these people (*are they people?*) watched me for some sort of reaction. I threw my hands up in the air.

"Okay, I have to go to bed. I have a show tomorrow. You all—I pointed at them—"can go wherever it is you go. I'm going to deal with this later. I can't do it right now."

I went to my bunk, brushing through the crowd, breaking up the fog among them. I climbed in and pulled my curtain closed.

What the fuck am I supposed to do now?

"Good morning Sam!" Amy said, and she shoved her hands through my bunk curtains to attack me.

"Jesus Christ, Amy!" I yelled. I almost fell out of the bunk, but was able to grab the ledge under my bunk and pull myself back in. Pulling my curtain back, I was met with her smiling face. I rolled my eyes, but smiled back. "You're going to kill me one day."

"Ah whatever. We'll make more money that way." A smug smile graced her face and I swatted at her.

"Oh fuck off. It's too early for death threats." I slid out of my bunk and got face to face with her. A shuddering sigh fell out of my mouth and I clung to Amy.

"Hey now, what's wrong?"

The images of the ghosts were painted on the inside of my eyelids. I couldn't escape them. My sleep had been restless, to say the absolute least. I shook my head. "It's hard to explain. I —" My words went dry.

"Whenever you want to talk about this, just come to me. We'll talk." She held me at arm's length and patted me on the back. "Now go brush your teeth. We have a day to start," she said lightly, and I gave her a half smile.

How am I ever going to explain this?

The morning slugged on. Tom, Amy, and I had a breakfast of instant grits and assorted fruit in the front of the bus. Every now and then, David would make a comment from the front about how bad the traffic was and the different roadkill he saw.

"So, tonight me and Sam are driving again," Amy said.

"Yeah. Last night wasn't as bad as I thought it was going to be, to be honest," Tom said.

"Well, I'm personally not hating our system here. Splitting the nights like this and alternating who goes first and second seems like a really solid plan. This way, no one will be too tired," Amy added.

I was staring out the window, wondering about the world. *If ghosts are real, what else is? Maybe mermaids. I could see that being a real thing.*

"Sam?"

"Huh?"

"I was asking if you're okay. You seem sort of out of it," Tom said.

I slouched down into the couch and realized that this was where Mark had sat last night. A chill ran over my spine and I tried to suppress it. I looked at my bandmates, my closest friends, and shook my head. "I'm fine, but we do need to talk later. Once we get to the venue, let's have a small band meeting."

Amy and Tom looked at each other for a moment and I clarified, "Nothing is wrong. We're all doing a great job. There's just something I need to tell you guys about and I don't want to do it while David is driving because I only want to say it once. Everything is okay."

Amy looked at me critically, but nodded anyway. Tom just nodded. I took a deep breath and nodded back.

"Well, I say we go to the back and play a game. Thoughts?" Tom proposed.

"Oh what, so you can beat my ass in Mario Kart again?" I asked with a smile.

"It doesn't have to be Mario Kart. I'll gladly beat your ass at any game."

I stood up and headed to the back. "Oh you're on, Baker."

The stage was set, the hair had been fixed, the warm-ups had been warmed up. Now it was time for my band meeting. I watched as Amy touched up her makeup in the mirror, clearly trying to look like she was busy for my sake. My nervousness was evident as I bounced from side to side, tangling my fingers together in a knot.

I sighed at my reflection in the mirror before feeling my voice leave my body. "Okay guys, quick band meeting." Everyone looked at me for a moment, before following my call to the small couch in our dressing room. I stood before the three of them, feeling like a lawyer trying to prove my case.

I didn't know how to start, so I just decided to blurt it out. "Our tour bus is haunted."

"What?!" David yelled. He jumped out of his seat and stood level with me. "So you *can* see ghosts! I knew it!"

I threw my hands up in defense. "It has nothing to do with me. Based on what they told me, all of us will be able to see them. At least on the bus, that is."

"So wait—how do you—how did you find this out?" Tom stuttered out.

I explained what happened and he looked stupefied.

"I mean, I do remember hearing some people in the back, but I figured it was you guys," Tom said, gesturing to Amy and David.

"I was dead asleep. I had to be ready to drive," David said.

"I was sleeping too." Amy said.

"Bullshit, I heard you playing Candy Crush, Amy," I said.

"Okay, yes, but after that I was asleep. Regardless, I wasn't in the kitchen."

Tom shook his head to himself for a moment. "So I heard ghosts talking?"

I nodded. "Yeah. I don't know why or how yet, but they seem to live there."

There was a knock at our door. It was our call to the stage.

"Let's try and worry about this later, okay? Remember the reason we even have the bus. Play hard, play true, play well."

It felt a bit like the Keep Calm and Carry On signs of World War II, but it seemed to work. Amy stood from the couch and shook out her limbs. David, already standing from his previous endeavor, jumped up and down a few times for good measure. Tom, admittedly, looked like he had seen a ghost, but he locked eyes with me and gave me a sure and steady nod despite himself.

"Okay. Let's do this."

Show three of our tour was much better than the one before. For the one thing, we were the second opener instead of the first, meaning that more people had trickled to their seats by the time we started. The nagging thoughts of the ghosts were pushed to the back of my mind as soon as I saw the several hundred people in front of us, waiting to be entertained.

"Hello Orlando! How's everyone doing tonight?" I shouted into the mic. There was a wave of cheers. "That's good to hear. Everyone, go ahead and give another hand to D Note Nation!" It's always the polite thing to acknowledge your bill-mates. You can only hope they'll do the same thing for you.

"Well, for those of you who don't know us, we are Approaching Grace and it's time for us to show you what we can do!" With that, the guys came in with a musical hit to officially mark the start of our set. Amy was riding her cymbals when I said, "Check this out." We started with one of our originals. We didn't have many, just over an album's worth.

We played three originals before we stopped for me to talk again.

"As you could probably tell, those were original songs, but you can't be an artist without having influences, so we're going to do a couple of covers right now. That way, we can show you who we are in terms that will be more familiar to you. We're going to start with a cover of 'Edge of Seventeen' by Stevie Nicks. I hope you enjoy it."

We played that song, to much fanfare, then followed it with a cover of "Daughters of Darkness" by Halestorm, and then concluded it with a cover of "Barracuda" by Heart. From there, we transitioned cleanly into another one of our originals. The crowd was on our side, clearly. Clapping, cheering loudly, and dancing. It was great. They were even accepting of the originals. By the time we got to the end of our set, the majority of the crowd was there in anticipation for the main event, but we had won them over too. We were on fire.

"Okay Orlando. I hate to say it, but we're at our last song."

There was negative feedback and I smiled. "I know! I hate it too! We've been having such an amazing time and we hope you have too. The only thing we can do now is send you off to the main event with a rocker! Right now, we're gonna do one of my favorite songs." Tom started the song and shock ran over the crowd as they realized that we were playing a song by Stadium. They started cheering louder than they had the entire time. I stretched my arms out to bask in the sound. "I think you know this one. This is 'Keep Coming Back' by Stadium. Let's go!"

The song started in earnest and I started dancing around the stage. David, Tom, and I had been running around the stage the whole time, keeping the energy up, but this was a bit different. This was purely for my enjoyment.

As I held my head back, drinking in the sound of the song, it hit me.

Stadium... The band whose career ended too soon due to a tragic bus accident in 1989. The band that was made up of Tommy "Blades" Tillen, Ronnie Guilder, Joey Rogers, and Mark Miller, aka Mark Stadium.

I stopped spinning and almost missed my cue to come in, but I didn't. I put on a bright smile, but in the back of my mind I was stunned.

We're not being haunted by just anyone. We're being haunted by Stadium.

We wrapped up the show nicely and we received a partial standing ovation. It would have been bliss if my mind hadn't just been blown. As we worked to break down the equipment and get ready to get back on the bus, I debated my options. *Do I tell the band who they are or do I let them just see it?* I hopped in one of the showers backstage. *I'm already pushing them by telling them ghosts are real. If I told them we're being haunted by our biggest inspiration, they'll never believe me.* By the time I got dressed, it was decided. *I'll let them find out for themselves.*

The plan for the night was for Amy and me to split the driving duty, however, the problem of introductions put a kink in our schedule. I didn't want them to do it alone and I didn't want us to get introduced separately. So, we decided to start down the road a bit and then stop at a rest area on the way to the next venue.

The time crawled slowly. I was supposed to be asleep in preparation for my shift, but I was nervous. *What if they don't show?* I sat in the back of the bus with David and Tom, who were watching *Back to the Future II*, one of my favorite movies, but I couldn't focus. Whether time crawled or jogged, I couldn't tell. I zoned out and then we were at the rest area. *Showtime.*

The bus parked and secure, we met Amy in the front of the bus. "Okay," she said. "Now what?" The three of them looked at me expectantly.

"I don't know. Last time, he just appeared." I looked around us. There was no fog in the cabin yet, so no one was here.

"Try calling out to them. That's what they always do in the movies," David suggested.

"We're really going to trust movies for how ghosts work? I'm pretty sure the guys from *Ghostbusters* didn't realize ghosts were actually real," Tom nagged.

David held his hands up defensively. "I'm sorry. I didn't realize you were the ghost expert all of a sudden."

The two of them fell into their usual spat of bickering when I heard a strange sound. It was like a woosh of air. Before I could turn around, I heard him.

"Hey guys, chill out. No one is a ghost expert, *especially* not us."

Tom and David stopped talking and Amy's jaw dropped. I turned around and there he was again in the fog with his leather and hairspray. Blades looked me up and down and smiled once, making me blush. *Why am I blushing? What the fuck is going on?*

"We haven't met yet," Blades continued. "My name is Blades, and I'm stuck on this bus with my bandmates." He gestured with his hand and the three other apparitions appeared, one by one.

"Is that—I mean, is he—?" Amy started, and Mark cut her off.

"Let's not do that. We'll introduce ourselves. We're still civilized," he said with a smile. "My name is Mark Miller. You may have known me as Mark Stadium."

Amy looked like she might faint. Tom didn't look much better. David, on the other hand...

"Oh my God! It's so great to meet you! My name is David, and can I just say that we are huge fans!" He stuck out his hand.

Mark smiled and looked at me for a moment before proceeding. "While I'm flattered, I'm afraid I can't accept your handshake." He gestured up and down to his spectral form. "The whole dead thing makes it pretty impossible to touch anything."

This seemed to intrigue David even more. He paused for a moment, looking down at his still-outstretched hand, and then asked, "What would happen if you tried?"

Mark chuckled a bit. He went to accept David's hand and, where there should have been a *clap* of two hands meeting, there was instead silence. Mark's hand passed through David's, seeming to dissipate for a moment before coming back together on the other side as if someone had disturbed a cloud of fog.

David's eyes lit up. "That's so cool. What else—"

"Okay, okay, we can interrogate their weirdness later. Let's get back to the point. Who are you and why are you here?" Tom asked.

"My name is Joey! I am—"

"The drummer," Amy said.

The blond man vibrated with energy. "Yes! And this is Ronnie." The other man was so quiet that he was barely noticeable up to this point. He didn't say anything when Joey introduced him; he didn't move aside from his eyes scanning over us. Joey spoke again, "I'm so glad that you know about us now so we can talk to you guys! It's been so boring to just talk to these guys for so long."

"So you're telling me that you are Stadium? *The* Stadium? The greatest songwriters of the last century? The minds behind 'Keep Coming Back,' 'Try Again,' and 'Make Me a Better Man'?" Amy paused, almost out of breath. She went on, slower this time. "The band that died in that horrific bus accident in 1989?"

Mark looked at his bandmates for a moment, then nodded.

Amy, in turn, looked back at me. "Sam said that this is your bus. So, this is the bus that you died in? Is it safe?"

"I want to tell you yes. I assume if it's still standing, that it's largely fine. We don't remember a lot of what happened that night," Blades said. His shoulders slumped a bit, though I wasn't sure if the others noticed it. "We don't know how or why we died."

"You don't remember?" David asked, and the guys shook their heads. "Oh wow."

I looked up at the clock in our living room. *It's getting late and we need to get on the road.* I looked over the whole group for a moment before heading up to the front and getting in the driver's seat. Their voices faded into the background as I started the bus up.

I put my head on the steering wheel for a second and closed my eyes. *What now?*

The bus traveled on through the night. We were headed for Fort Lauderdale, only a few hours from Orlando. Our plan was that once we got there, we would stop at another rest area for me to sleep for the night before going on to the venue.

When we stopped at the second rest area of the night, I got up and stretched. My band was asleep in the living room, clearly having fallen asleep while talking to our new neighbors. I sighed before going to the back to grab some blankets. I covered them up before heading to the back once again to get comfortable, myself. As I stretched out on the couch, Blades appeared next to me.

"Hey," he said.

"Hey. What's up?" *When do you get used to talking to the dead?*

He adjusted the hat on his head. "I was just checking on you. Your bandmates are asleep. Mine are resting as well."

"You need to sleep?"

"Think of it more like charging up, but yeah. We need to rest."

I nodded for a moment. "Why aren't you there, then?"

"I told you. I wanted to check on you." The hat came off now and I could get a better look at him. The hat cast a shadow on his soft, sad gray-blue eyes. Now they were apparent. He set the hat on the couch next to him. "I also had a proposition."

I sat up on my elbow. "Go on."

"I know this is very shocking for all of you and I feel a bit bad about it. I mean, it's not like we could help it. We're stuck here. But, I still feel like a bit of a burden for you guys. So, I wanted to propose a sort of trade."

"A trade?"

"Yes, in a manner of speaking. Your bandmates gave up the fact that we were one of your favorite bands. They also mentioned that you're a bit slow when it comes to the song-writing process."

"Hey now. It's not easy to write something completely new out of nowhere—"

He put his hands up defensively, but smiled. "I knew you reminded me of Mark." He put his hands down. "It is very hard to write a song, which is where my offer comes in. We weren't exactly done with our career when we died. We were just getting started. I've been stuck on this bus for almost thirty years with the most creative people I know. And we have no way to get it out."

"What are you saying?"

"We want to write with you, get our ideas out of our heads and onto paper. It's not like we can hold pencils or anything. And maybe, if you like any of it, you can even get it onto vinyl."

I stifled a chuckle.

"What?"

"No one really does vinyl anymore."

His face scrunched up. "Is everything just on the radio now, then?"

This time I laughed. "No. You know what? In exchange for your writing help, we'll explain modern technology for you. Is that a deal?"

He smiled, "Deal."

"Okay great. Can I go to sleep now?"

"Sure thing." He placed his hat back on his head, once again covering his sad eyes, and then vanished.

I shook my head and tucked myself in on the couch, but when I closed my eyes, all I could see were those sad ones.

Home at Last

THE WAY I structured that first tour was very purposeful. I knew that we weren't equipped to be on the road for very long stretches of time. We just simply didn't have the manpower or the resources or the gas money. So after a month, we headed back home for a bit so the guys could go back to work and we could write and record more for the album we wanted to put out at the end of the year. And so we pulled into the driveway, everything having gone according to plan, except...

"You'll have to get back on the bus for your writing sessions so we can help you!" Joey said, his cloud puffing up as he jumped.

"I promise you, we'll come back if we need any help," Amy said.

"Come more often than that! Remember, no one can see us outside of the bus." Joey pouted.

Amy rolled her eyes and smiled. "You'll be fine. You've

been alone for much longer than a month before. After this month, we're getting back on the bus. It'll be okay."

Joey opened his mouth to protest, but Mark clamped his hand over it. "We'll be fine. It just gets so boring to hang out here alone, so we are going to hang out around you guys. You won't be able to tell."

"I can live with that. Hey, if we start writing something really dumb, just flicker the lights or something," I chimed in, unloading my bag from the bunk hall.

"We'll try our best," Blades said. He had one of his shit-eating grins on his face, about what I had no clue.

"I doubt we'll be able to since we can't touch stuff. But, who knows, maybe that'll change," Mark said with a shrug.

With that, we said our goodbyes and headed inside our house with all of our stuff.

"Home sweet home," David said.

"It would be even sweeter if you had taken the trash out before we left. It smells like shit in here," Tom said.

"I'll take care of it right now," David proclaimed, as if it made up for his previous transgression. Tom shook his head and headed up the stairs to put up his stuff. Amy and I carried our equipment into the living room so it could be put in the basement later.

"So do you think they're actually watching us?" Amy asked.

"I don't think they'd lie about it. I doubt they're watching our every move or anything." I sat down on the couch and Amy joined me. I looked at the ceiling. "But, for the record, if you guys are here, do *not* follow us into the bathrooms or anything. That's creepy as hell and we'll be mad if we find out about it."

"Oh God, that's creepy. I was going to take a shower right now, but now I have that in my head." Her body shook with a mock shiver and I laughed.

"See guys? Don't do it." We both laughed at that.

It's good to be home.

"Okay, and what do you think about this lyric next: 'And if you'd let me, I'd never leave you'?"

"I'm not sure, Sam. That feels a bit redundant to me," Tom said.

"It does sort of repeat the line from the first verse, doesn't it?" I stared at the notebook in my hand and groaned. While David and Amy were at work, Tom and I had been working on the lyrics for this one song all morning and weren't really getting anywhere.

Tom stood up. "I don't know about you, but I'm just about ready to call it quits for today." He looked around our dark basement for a moment and sighed. "I'm going to go make a sandwich and then I'll be back down."

"Maybe a break is exactly what we need." I looked back down at the notebook and sighed myself. "I'll be up in a few minutes. Don't use all of the peanut butter."

He smiled at my comment and went upstairs.

"Now, why can't I get this to work? It's not usually this hard." I set my head down on the coffee table in front of me. "Okay, maybe it is usually this hard."

"What if it went: 'And if you'd let me, I'd never let you go'?"

I shot upright. "Blades? How are you here?"

The apparition smiled at me. "I knew you'd be able to see us. Something about you is different." He shrugged as if this wasn't a huge revelation to me.

I searched for words but my mouth just sat agape in shock.

"Okay guys, she can see us. Come on down," Blades called,

and suddenly the rest of Stadium was with me in the basement.

"How is this possible?" I asked.

"Oh, we have no idea, really," Mark said. "I'm just happy this worked. I have some ideas for the song…"

And so we went along with Mark helping me write the song. Blades tossed in a word here or there while Joey and Ronnie explored our basement studio. By the time Tom came back down the stairs, thirty or so minutes later, the song was complete.

"Make any headway?" he asked, handing me a peanut butter and jelly sandwich on a plate.

"Thank you and, I think you'll be surprised. I know I am," I said, and handed him the notebook.

"You finished it?"

"Not without a little help." I looked around at the guys sprawled out on our couches.

Tom followed my gaze and frowned. "Can you see them? Are they here?" I nodded and he asked, "Well, how can *you* see them if I can't?"

I shrugged. "I honestly have no idea. I'm going to do some research online later to see if I can find anything that makes sense, but I really don't know. I mean, why can't *you* see them? What makes us different from each other?"

Tom's face was troubled still, but he looked down at the notebook in his hands, reading the lyrics. "If we can keep coming up with stuff like this, I don't care how you do it. Just keep doing it."

It wasn't until I heard Amy come home that I realized how long I had been in my room. The light from the window had gone down with the sun and my room was now solely lit by my laptop. Blades was sitting next to me on my bed, staring in wonderment at my laptop.

"What are you doing up here all alone?" Amy said, coming in and sitting at the end of my bed.

I looked at Blades. "I'm trying to find out why I can see ghosts."

"We can all see the ghosts. I hate to say it, but it's the bus that's special, not us."

I hesitated for a moment. I looked at my laptop and then Blades, who I realized was grinning at the old Stadium posters on my walls. I sighed. "Can you see him?"

Amy's eyebrows scrunched up and she looked around. "Who are you talking about?"

"This is my point. Blades is sitting right here," I said, gesturing to the spirit beside me.

"You can see him?"

"I can hear him too. Him and Mark came to me in the basement and helped me write some lyrics. Tom couldn't see them either."

"And so you've been trying to figure out *why* you can see them and we can't. That's a fair question. Have you found anything?"

I showed her my laptop and the document I had put together. As her eyes skimmed the pages, I saw that Blades had moved closer to me. Instead of sitting a bit away from me on the bed as he had been when we started our search, I found that he was now right next to me. *When did this happen?* He seemed quite content with his position, watching Amy to gauge her reaction to our hours of work. I tore my eyes away from the soft indent of a dimple on the right side of his mouth and joined him in looking at Amy.

"Well, I don't think you're a fairy or medium or anything like that," she said, handing me back the laptop.

"Last time I checked, I didn't have any wings."

"Maybe we should check again," Blades said, and I whipped around to look at him. He was wearing that little shit-eating grin of his again and I could do nothing but roll my eyes.

"What just happened?" Amy asked.

I shook my head. "Blades thinks he's funny." She gestured for me to go on. "It's not relevant. Let's get back to the important question: Why can I see dead people?"

"You're like the kid from *Sixth Sense*!"

"David? When did *you* get here?"

"Oh, I've been standing here a few minutes," he said, walking into my room. He was still dressed in his uniform from the coffee shop. "And just for the record, I told you so."

"About what?"

He gestured incredulously at me. "What do you mean, about what? About seeing ghosts! I called it during the first tour, after you got shocked."

"Holy shit," Amy said.

The room went silent. Even the air seemed to still, as no one moved. "You're right, David," I said, and he beamed.

"Feel free to say that again."

I shook my head at him and started typing furiously on my laptop. Amy got up and stood next to the bed, looking over my shoulder as I searched. "This says, 'Some people claim that they saw visions of God and Heaven when they were electrocuted, others Hell or Satan. Some people claim that they felt as though they actually died before being brought back by doctors.'"

"Well, what did you see?" Amy asked.

I thought back to that night in the bar. I could feel the anger surging inside of me as I pulled out those cables and I could feel my finger slipping between the prongs as I pulled. The electricity flowed through me, touching every part of me before coming back and circling again, endlessly. It was an eternity, but... "I saw nothing."

David slouched from his new position at the end of the bed. "Well, what does that mean?"

"That's what I saw too," Blades said. "When I first died, I saw nothing. I always thought I'd see the Pearly Gates or even fire and brimstone, but there was nothing. Just darkness."

"Do you think I died?" My voice was barely a whisper. I wasn't sure if I even spoke until David tried to respond.

"I mean—"

"Be quiet, David. She's asking him," Amy said.

Blades chuckled in amusement for a moment before falling into a sullen mood. "I have no way of knowing for sure. I only know what I have experienced for myself and what the other guys have told me about what they saw."

I stared at my computer screen for a second before taking a shaking hand to the keyboard and typing *Can you die from electrical shock?* I held my breath. It seemed as though everything was silent, though I knew that David was talking in the background. The screen loaded forever and I hung on that spinning circle like a girl strapped to the wheel of death. After a brief eternity, the answer was plain. *Yes.*

"That makes perfect sense. You died for a bit, but came back, and now you can see ghosts. That's awesome!" David said.

I stared at the screen. *I died. I literally died and I saw nothing. What does this mean?*

Now faced with the concepts of my own mortality and new supernatural abilities, I was full of songs. It seems that finding out you died can really be inspiring. Hey, it worked for Nikki Sixx. Plus, with the help of Stadium, songs were getting pumped out daily. While the guys were working, I would spend my mornings writing with Stadium and my afternoons laying down basic tracks for recording. Productivity was me and I was productivity. It was glorious. When the guys came home from work, they'd lay their tracks on each song and by the end of the month, we had more than enough songs to fill a full record.

There were other developments during this time as well. And if you'll indulge me, I'd like to relive them. Once again we venture into the thick of it.

"That's a wrap on song four. I know Tom will love this one. Perfect guitar song."

"One hundred percent. I wish I could play on it," Blades said.

I smiled. "Now that would be something. 'Ms. Roland, care to tell us who's on this song?' 'Oh, just some dead people.'"

Blades laughed and moved to stand up from the couch. "Break time, I assume?"

"Yep. Time for a *Family Ties* marathon." I started up the stairs slowly. "See you there?" He smirked at me and vanished from sight. I rolled my eyes and continued up the stairs. He sat on the couch, waiting for me. I grabbed the remote and turned on the TV before stepping into the kitchen to make a sandwich.

"I can't believe that people still watch this show."

I peeked my head out from the kitchen and saw him standing next to the TV. *Probably admiring how thin it is.* I smiled to myself and picked up my plate to carry into the living room. "Well, it's not like everyone watches it. It took me forever to find it on streaming."

"I also still can't believe you can watch whatever you want, whenever you want."

I sat down on the couch, "We do live in the future, sometimes. The fact that we can do this, but can't fly..."

He smirked at me as he sat down. "They *did* tell us that you'd have flying cars."

I shrugged and looked at the TV. "Seems like they promised you a lot of things that didn't come true." We watched the show, and it wasn't for a while that I noticed he had his arm around my shoulders. *He can't touch me, but he sure is trying.* I smiled at this for a moment and attempted to lean into the space that wouldn't hold me.

Back on the Road Again

WITH OUR DEBUT album sent off to be mixed, there was nothing else for us to do but to get back on the road. Our first leg took us from North Carolina to Florida, but this leg was going to take us up the East Coast. As we packed our stuff up once again, I couldn't help but feel that *this* was how life was supposed to be. This epic ode to travel and endless showcasing of our music was the ideal, the goal, the dream that I (and all of us) had been set to capture this whole time. Everything was right in the world.

"SOS guys! I have an emergency!"

I ran from where I was packing in my room to David's down the hall. "What's wrong? What's the emergency?"

"My bass broke."

"What do you *mean* your bass broke? You're supposed to just be packing," Tom said, coming in behind me.

Behind David, in the corner of his room, stood Ronnie.

"Yeah, he really broke it, Sam. I was there and even I'm not exactly sure what happened."

I frowned at the ghost and turned back to David, who sat cradling his bass like a wounded child. "What are you going to do?"

He stared at his dearly departed for a moment before sighing. "I have a backup bass."

"A backup bass?"

"A backup bass. It's at my mom's house."

Tom lightly tossed his hands in the air. "Oh that's not bad. We can just stop there on the way out."

David shook his head for a moment, but said, "Yeah, that's probably the best idea."

We arrived at David's house a few hours later.

"It's really weird that we haven't been here before," Amy said. "I mean, we've known you forever."

"You'll see why in a moment," David said and rang the doorbell.

The door opened revealing an older woman with dark brown hair, holding a dish towel, "I'm not interested in buying anything," she said without looking at us.

"Mamá, it 's me."

"David? Mi vida! You should have called. Adelante," she said, and ushered all of us inside. The house was decorated with gorgeous art, surrounded by elaborate tapestries. We followed her into the living room and sat on ornate couches that seemed unfit for actual sitting.

"Are you guys hungry? I could make something real quick—"

"Mamá, don't worry about it. I just came to get my other bass."

"¿Por qué? What happened to the last one?"

"It broke, Mama. Don't worry about it—"

"¡Ay dios mío! It broke? Eres tan torpe. You're always breaking everything." She shook her head in displeasure and left the room.

"Okay—this is my moment. I'm going to go upstairs and grab my bass. I'll be back." David dashed out of the room at a frightening pace.

"Alone again, naturally," Amy said, and I chuckled.

David's mom came back in the room with a plate of assorted foods. "Here, eat." She set the plate down in front of us.

After a few moments, David came back down the stairs, bass in hand. He saw us eating off the plate of food and rolled his eyes. "Mamá! I told you not to worry about it."

"Ah, mi vida. It's no problem. You sit and eat too."

"We have to leave, Mamá."

"No you don't. I haven't seen you in months. So you're going to sit here and eat with your mother."

We shared a knowing look and a smile at David's anguish.

Three hours later, we were out of the house and on the road, but not without David receiving a chiding for not visiting, an invitation to us to come again, and a plate of food wrapped in tin foil.

"Your mom is really nice," Amy called from the driver's seat.

"That's what you think. You don't speak Spanish," David replied from the couch, changing the strings on the new bass.

I stared out the window, watching the highway speeding past us. The sky was bright blue, a good omen considering the outside location of our gig the next day. We were headed to

Virginia, but the short duration of the trip meant we were going to make a stop first. We just had to decide where.

"We should go to Virginia Beach."

"The last time we went to the beach, you got too sunburned to move," David said, and I shrugged.

"It was worth it."

"We should try to stay indoors so we aren't tired for the show tomorrow. We could go to a museum. Ooh—or an aquarium!" Amy called from the front.

"We've been to tons of aquariums, Ams. They're all the same. We can just do that at home," I said.

"But what if they have cool native fish?"

"The difference in wildlife from North Carolina to Virginia really can't be that different. We won't be missing much," I said, rolling my eyes.

Tom mumbled something.

"What did you say?"

"What about Colonial Williamsburg?"

"Really? That nerd spot?" David said, aghast. "I wouldn't be caught dead there."

The bus pulled up in the parking lot of Colonial Williamsburg a few hours later. David sat stewing in his own displeasure; Amy was satisfied, her desire for a museum met with this location choice; and Tom was vibrating with joy. We got off the bus and headed to the entrance.

"We could go to the blacksmith shop. Ooh! Or the apothecary. Or—we could go to the harpsichord maker!"

"Let's go there, Tom," I said.

The usually silent guitarist all but squealed in joy, clacked his heels together, and did a somersault. With an extra pep in his step, he led us to the location as indicated on his map. I shook my head and followed him, Amy jogging to catch up and David trudging behind.

The day went on in that fashion, with us trailing behind

Tom's eager footsteps. We must have done everything there. The day, while fun, was pretty unremarkable, until—

"Oh my gosh. Are you who I think you are?"

Our little group spun around slowly.

"You are!" The voice came from a younger guy, probably no older than fifteen. "I can't believe it's you. What are you doing here?"

"I'm sorry—are you talking to us?" Amy asked.

"Of course! You guys *are* Approaching Grace, right?" We stood silent for a moment and he pointed at each of us. "Tom Baker. David Perry. Amy Collins. Samantha Roland. It's you!"

"Yeah, you've caught us," I said with a shaky smile.

"I love your band. 'Give Me A Chance' is one of my all-time favorite songs!"

I looked at the other guys with shock. *That song hasn't even been released yet. How has he heard it? How has he heard us at all?*

"Oh wow. Thank you," Amy said, and extended a hand for him to shake.

He accepted it gladly and then turned to me. "What are you guys doing here? Are you playing somewhere?"

"We're playing in the Blue Ridge Festival tomorrow at four."

"That's awesome! I hope I can still get a ticket." He paused for a moment and swayed on his feet. "Could I possibly get a selfie?"

"Sure!" I said, and we crowded together with him for the photo. He took a few and then stepped away. "What's your name, kid?"

"John! Nice to meet you!"

"Nice to meet you too, John. I hope we'll see you at the show tomorrow."

"Me too! Thanks again! I can't wait to post these online."

He pulled himself away from us. "I'll be sure to tag you guys!" he shouted as he jogged off somewhere.

I looked at my bandmates with a smug grin. "Well fellas. I think we're officially famous."

Don't Go Away Mad (Just Go Away)

THE REVIEWS of our first album trickled in slowly. It wasn't a huge album, at least not at first. About six months after the release, it got picked up by a major music reviewer by the name of Shaun Greensby. We were on tour still, finally conquering the West Coast, when we found out. Overnight, plays of our album skyrocketed and the following weeks saw an explosion in reviews, largely positive. The increased attention on the album also meant that there were more people coming to shows to see *us*, in addition to the headliner, which was amazing. We were elated beyond comparison and so it was time to plan, again.

"We need to get back in the studio ASAP," David said.

I reached over the table at the diner and adjusted his baseball cap, pulling it into place on his head. "I agree with you. I've been writing some stuff with Mark, so we can hop on it as soon as we want to."

"Good," David said, and I replied with a curt nod.

"Don't you think the hats and sunglasses make you look *more* suspicious? You *are* inside," Blades said to me, and I grimaced.

"If anything, my talking to dead people makes me more of a sideshow attraction than my apparel," I whispered.

He chuckled. "You might be onto something there."

"Blades giving you flak again?" Tom asked.

I nodded and grabbed a knife to spread cream cheese on the bagel that had arrived at our table.

We all dug into our breakfast, our chatter slowing as we focused on our nourishment. I looked at the diner around us, taking note of the mural on the wall. It depicted the Golden Gate Bridge basking in the yellow and orange glow of the sunrise on one side and cloaked in the red and purple veil of the sunset on the other. It was a familiar sight to the locals, who could simply gaze out the window and see the very art that was on the wall. The brevity of our trip meant that sightseeing would be largely out of the question.

"We only have a month left of this tour, then we can go back to the studio," Amy said, and I nodded, returning my mind back to the table.

"Let's record it and then shop it around a bit. I bet we would get some label to bite at it," David suggested.

"For once, I agree with you," Tom said, knocking David's hat off playfully.

I saw Amy shift in her seat, so I took another bite of my bagel as she stirred. "I don't know, guys. I still think a label might be more trouble than it's worth," she said. No one spoke, so she continued. "I mean, look at what happened to Tom Petty or Queen or even Night Ranger. All a label seems to be good for is extortion and creative limitation."

The table slumped a bit at this. They were good points, but dangerous ones, so the topic shifted.

"We don't have to decide anything right now. Besides," I

said, looking at my watch, "we need to be heading back soon if we want any chance of getting a soundcheck."

We quickly stuffed down the food, paid, and went back to the venue.

Our dressing room was small—we *were* the opener, after all—but it was actually split into two separate rooms, which was a nice touch. Amy, Tom, and David were in one room and I was in the other ("Well, I'm the one who has to deal with all the dead people following me around. There's three of you in there, but five of us in here. Just let me have this"). I stepped out of the shower, quickly wrapping a towel around myself. *Just because I don't see them doesn't mean—*

"What, no show?"

"Jesus Christ, Blades."

His body joined his voice in the room, his freshly appeared face showing that same shit-eating grin. "No, it's just me," Blades said. "That'd be crazy though." He watched me step back behind the shower curtain to towel off. "Hey, could you see Jesus? He is the Holy *Ghost*, right?"

I stuck my head out of the shower, "If I can, I haven't yet."

"So does that mean—"

"I'm not answering that."

"That's fair."

I got back out of the shower, now dry, and walked over to my road case to grab some clothes. Then, checking that there were no mirrors, I stepped behind the case to get dressed. Pulling a shirt over my head, I leaned back out to look at Blades, who was checking out the nondescript art on the walls. "What's on your mind?"

"Hm?" He spun around and locked eyes with me, his smile twitching. "How did you know?"

I zipped my pants and stepped into the body of the room. I grabbed a pair of shoes and sat down to put them on. "Well, you only made one nudity joke, so something must be wrong."

He scoffed. "Sam, I am a man of stature. I'm no animal."

"Sure," I said, unconvinced, but I looked at him with soft eyes.

He looked at me again and sighed, taking a seat next to me. "I heard you guys talking last night about the next tour. You said that you were going to try to headline and—" His voice caught for a moment and he paused. His gray-blue eyes didn't meet mine. "I don't think it's a good idea."

I stiffened. "What? Why?"

He shook his head slightly. "I just don't think you're ready."

I stood up abruptly.

"Now, hold on a moment, Sam," he continued as I grabbed my makeup kit and hair tools. Blades stood and walked over to me. "You're just so new. I'm not sure if you could sell it. I'd hate to see you be disappointed and I'm not sure if you have the following to support it—"

I walked out of my dressing room and went into the other one. Amy, Tom, and David stopped in their tracks, obviously caught off guard by my entrance. I quickly closed the door behind me, caring just enough to make sure I didn't slam it and disturb the other acts. Tom and David resumed their action, clearly taking the "step away" approach to my visible anger. Amy, on the other hand, noticed my glassy eyes and red face. She set her drumsticks down on her practice pad and came over to hug me.

"What happened?" she whispered in my ear.

I shook my head, squeezing her tighter. "Later."

She nodded on my shoulder and continued to hold me. Behind her, I saw Blades standing in the middle of the room, unnoticed by the others. I glared at him before nuzzling my face into the space where Amy's neck and shoulder met and when we eventually pulled apart, he was gone.

The month was up quickly and very soon we were driving back to Fortress Grace (the name of our home) on the other coast. It was a straight drive from Washington state to North Carolina, a monster of a trip that we had decided to split up into day-long shifts. We would stop at night to sleep to make it a little less painful. Day two was my first turn on the trek and I was trucking along, lost in thought. The radio played one of my driving playlists at a medium volume and I could hear David and Amy playfully arguing over their favorite movies in the living room.

I hadn't seen Blades since that night in San Francisco, but I wasn't complaining. My grip on the wheel tightened as I thought of the interaction. *He thinks we're not ready, that I'm not ready. We just did a whole nationwide tour, but we're not ready. Our album is on the charts, the actual rock charts. We have almost a million followers online. He doesn't understand. He'll never understand.* A Stadium song came on and I groaned, reaching to hit the skip button.

"Hey, I like this one."

I jolted in my seat, still slightly unnerved by the sudden voices that liked to come out of nowhere all the time. "What do you want, Mark?"

He appeared in the seat next to me. "I heard you and Blades had a spat a few weeks ago."

I scoffed. "Oh, it's no big deal. He just invalidated my whole career."

"I see." He fell silent, but not in a cruel way. It was clear he was waiting for me to speak.

I gave into his silent request and spoke. "Why are you bringing this up now?"

I saw him shrug out of the corner of my eye. "No reason."

The song played on in our silence. When it hit the guitar solo, I tensed, then relaxed. *Damn you, Blades.*

Mark must've seen my reaction. "I know the feeling. Hard to be mad when he is such a damn good guitar player."

I chuckled in spite of myself. "It really is a shame what happened to you guys. Just think of what you could've made with more time." I glanced at him briefly, catching his nod and the melancholy on his face.

"I wish I could remember what happened that night."

"You really don't remember anything?"

"Not at all."

I looked at the highway in front of us, miles and miles of the same, never-ending pavement. Beyond it was a similarly endless desert, peppered with cacti and sparse plants.

"I remember that night, but at the end of it, we just woke up dead, essentially," he said.

"Oh wow."

"Yeah."

"What do you remember of that day?"

"I won't bore you with the details, but I will tell you this —we were on our first headlining tour."

The next song came on in the playlist, but I didn't hear it at first. Mark's words settled in my stomach like a heavy meal. I swallowed uncomfortably. "*Oh.*"

On the side of the road were two cars. The driver of the first car was getting out with what looked to be a tool bag.

"You have to understand, I'm not defending Blades. He can be an absolute ass, but he cares about people." I saw the driver help the second driver start to change a tire on the car and then they were out of view, just another blur on the highway. "And he cares about you."

I sat in stunned silence, trying to focus on the road ahead of me.

Mark cleared his throat. "By the way, we were recording an album at the time too. We were going to finish it at the end of that leg of the tour."

"So, in a studio somewhere in LA is a partially completed third Stadium album?"

"Mhm."

"Damn."

"Yeah."

Since our album was already written on the road, it didn't take long for us to record and finish it. It was even faster this time, since the guys didn't have to go to work due to our increased revenue from the tour.

I hit the stop button on the track. "Great job, Tom. Do you think you could do another take with less emphasis on the pentatonics?" He gave a thumbs up and I hit record on a new track.

Amy and David sat on the couch behind me, listening intently through clunky headphones. Amy's elbows were on her knees, head down between her legs like she was sheltering from a storm. David was stretched out, taking up the space Amy had surrendered. Both of them had their eyes closed. Tom hit a golden stretch of notes on the guitar and I clapped once before moving my hands in excitement. David jumped up and thrust his fist in the air, and Amy's head shot up, her face plastered with a broad smile. The section came to an end and I hit "stop" again. Tom looked at me through the glass window and I motioned for him to come into the mixing room.

"How was that?" he asked, and I smiled.

The Best of Times

WE SPENT the next three months planning, preparing, and playing. We used our little old van as opposed to our treasured bus to save some gas money as we drove around North Carolina, South Carolina, Tennessee, and Virginia to do short stints at different venues. Each crowd was bigger than the last and even more into the music we were playing. It was all the encouragement we needed to start booking dates for a head-lining tour to coincide with the release of our second album, which we had decided to call, *Approaching Grace: Getting Closer*.

But before we could go on tour, it was decided that we should get some photos done for promotional purposes.

On a humid October day, we headed to the photo studio for the shoot.

"Why did we choose today? The humidity is mucking up my hair," David said. He was staring at himself intently in the passenger side visor mirror.

"It's humid every day till winter, David. What do you want me to do about it?" Tom said from the driver's seat.

"It could be worse. It could be raining," Amy added.

"Gah, don't say that!" David whipped around to look at the both of us. "Now it's gonna rain."

I rolled my eyes and smiled. "It'll be all right. We're going to get touched up when we get there anyway."

He closed the mirror and folded up the visor. "Fine."

I stifled my chuckle and looked out the window. *Beautiful day to be a rock star.*

"Okay, I'm going to put on your album and you feel free to just move. Dance around, jump up and down, do whatever you feel. We'll photograph around you," Bryan, the shoot supervisor, said.

We were dressed up like we were going on stage. We were leathered and glittered up, my hair had been teased up some, and Amy was wearing heels (a shoot exclusive). I felt like Axl Rose and I loved it. The album came on with a bang as "Slide on Up" started.

"Hell yeah!" Amy said, and started playing air guitar. I laughed and mirrored her, crouching a bit beside her. David started air drumming along, bobbing his head and biting his lip like Amy does. As the verse came in, Tom mimed walking up to a mic stand and started singing along with my tracked voice,

"Oh yeah, boy—just slide up on me—" He paused at the end of the line to prim up his hair and pull up his pants.

"Oh my God, do I do that?" I shouted over the music, mortified. David nodded, laughing. I was riddled with giggles as we transitioned from miming each other to dancing—Tom and Amy and David and I. We dipped and spun and jumped and stomped and made great fools of ourselves.

The album pressed on and we kept going. David climbed on Tom's back, sending them both to the floor. Amy made kissy faces at the camera. The guys grabbed me and lifted me in the air. Amy and I pretended to make out while Tom and David "fought" in the background. We spun and spun and spun before collapsing to the ground. And as we laid there, out of breath, Bryan was taking photos of us. We were laughing and smiling. We'd forgotten we weren't alone.

The album was paused towards the end and we all stumbled up off the floor. We were still laughing, but once we stopped I started again. In the corner was a stationary camera filming our every absurd movement.

"Oh no," Amy said, and dropped her head in her hands, laughing again.

"Oh yes! We're definitely using that for the marketing," I replied with a wide grin.

"Dammit, Sam," Tom said, but his eyes were smiling.

"What?" I asked, and they laughed at me.

Bryan came over and showed us some of the photos. We'd done it. Our first real rock star photoshoot was complete.

We used those photos for all of the promo for "Getting Closer." They were everywhere. And that video of the shoot ended up online a while later and has over 35 million views at the time I'm writing this book. In fact, the shoot was so successful that the album cover was the shot of all of us laying on the ground, almost stacked on top of each other. We were grinning wildly, bright teeth and scrunched noses. Reviewers have said some nonsense about the cover "bleeding rock and roll," but I think it was more than that. Sure, we were dressed in our rock garb, but our faces were earnest. We were just so happy to be there and that joy is what actually bled onto the cover. We were ecstatic. We were bigger than we'd ever thought we could be, realistically. And we were only going to get bigger.

The album came out on November twelfth and we were in Raleigh for the release party show. Our opening act was another local band we had found on Instagram called Butterfly Eyes. They were a young group, like us, who played rock music, though they mixed it with some funk for flavor. Butterfly Eyes were set to be on our bill for the first month of our tour and then we would officially be on our own. In addition to the new opening act, our company had grown significantly with a crew and, finally, a bus driver. We met up with the crew at Fortress Grace and our tour bus parade departed for Raleigh early in the morning. Mike, our bus driver, made himself known early on.

"Okay kids. My name is Mike. Not Michael, not Mikey— Mike. I have been driving buses for longer than you've been alive and I feel like it."

I raked my eyes over his figure. He was a decently tall man, certainly taller than me, with a round face and a wide, flat nose. He had a receding hairline of light brown hair that matched a similarly colored horseshoe-style mustache.

Mike went on, "My back hurts, my neck hurts, my everything hurts, so you better know that if we don't jive, I won't drive."

We all sat in the bus on the front couches and stared at him up at his standing figure attentively. I gave Amy a side-eye for a moment as Mike continued.

"It is my job to get you where you need to be. It's your job to let me do my job. That means no crazy partying, no drugs, and no nonsense. If you want to do any of that shit, feel free to find another driver 'cause I ain't your guy. Understand?" He gave a singular, strong pat to his round stomach, as if to punctuate his point. It was then that I noticed the Lynyrd Skynyrd shirt he was wearing, along with a leather vest, dark blue jeans, and an appropriately large belt buckle to match.

We nodded hesitantly and a smile crawled across his face. "Then we should get along just fine. Now come on. We've got a show tonight."

Mike went to the front and we were off. The band stared at each other and then we broke out laughing.

"So," David said with a giggle, "when do we tell him about the ghosts?"

"He'll find out sooner or later on his own. Let's let him figure it out," Tom said. We came into an easy calm, like that before a storm. We were on our way.

***

We were led down the corridor, one we had been down a few times before when we had been an opening act, but we turned a corner past our old dressing room and went down a new hallway.

"These two rooms are for you, so feel free to split them up as you please—it's up to you guys. There are signs in the hallway that will lead you to catering, the stage, and anywhere else you might need to go. There are also schedules out there."

"All right, thank you," Amy said. Our tour guide nodded once before vanishing back down the hall. We split the rooms between Amy and me, and David and Tom. As we waited for our road cases to come ("It should only take a few minutes," she had said), Amy and I discussed things.

"So, I haven't seen Blades in a while," she started.

"I hadn't noticed," I said.

She looked at me, one eyebrow cocked up. "Uh huh. Well, I know you're still mad at him, but he can't stay in that spirit realm forever, right? Besides, it's been over four months, Sam."

She *was* right, of course. That didn't change my mind, though. "He's welcome to come back out whenever he wants to, but I'm not calling for him. Besides, I hear him talking to Mark at night, so he must be fine—just avoiding me. And all of us, I guess."

The door opened and a member of our crew rolled in our two cases.

"Thanks, Joel," Amy said. To me, she added, "It's up to you, Sam. It's your relationship. I'm not going to get in the way."

My breath caught in my throat as I struggled to force out, "We're not in a relationship." *Is it that obvious?*

"Uh huh. Then why are you so mad? You have dealt with criticism from all grades of people over the years. You wouldn't be so hurt if you didn't value his opinion so much." She stood up. "I'm going to scope out the stage and check out my drums before sound check. Want to join me?"

I shook my head, "No, I want to get a head start on my makeup. I'll see you later."

"Suit yourself," she said with a shrug.

The door closed with a click behind her and I sighed. *I guess I'm not hiding my feelings as well as I thought. But he hurt me, hurt my pride, my confidence.*

I looked around the room. There was a full wall mirror surrounded by light bulbs in a picture perfect setup on the left wall. On the right wall was a plush white couch. The next wall had a shower area.

I can't let him, or my feelings for him, get in the way of my success. As I spun around the room, I felt the weight of eyes on me. "Can I help you?" I asked.

"Nah. I'm just here to bug you." I turned around and met Blades' eyes. He wore a shy smile.

I rolled my eyes. "You want to bug me now? In just a few hours, thousands of people are going to file into that arena to see the first show of our first headlining stadium tour and you want to bother me now?" I grabbed my makeup bag out of my road case.

"Okay fine, I wanted to talk to you. I have something I want to say."

Without turning around, I started, "Why are you here?" I went about setting my makeup up on the long table in front of the mirror, arranging everything to my specific way.

"I told you, I needed to speak to you."

I stood my foundation, eyeliner, mascara, mascara primer, and setting spray up at the top of my workspace. Then I rolled out my brushes and arranged them in height order. "Blades, I haven't seen you in months. I know you're pissed at me. Why else would you be avoiding me so much?" I kept my eyes down on my work, pulling out my eyeshadow palettes, opening and closing them to determine which ones I would need for the night. *Maybe if I keep going, he will leave and this will all be over. Maybe he will never talk to me again.* I felt my heart drop into my stomach, but I put on my mean face to brave through it.

"Sam, I was trying to give you space. I knew that you didn't want to see me, so I stopped showing up."

I assigned my brushes to the eyeshadows I wanted and paused. My routine was complete. *Now I have to deal with him.* I sighed. "Can we just cut to the part where you tell me why this is a bad idea?" I waved my arms halfheartedly, still staring at my makeup. "We all know that you think the band isn't ready for this tour, you made sure that I knew that. And those words have been stuck in my head for months, haunting me just like you do." I heard the words after I said them and I paused for a moment. *You can do this.* I continued, "Better yet, can we talk about it *after* our biggest show yet?"

"That's why I came, I'm trying to tell you—"

I cut him off. "And another thing—"

"Sam, I love you."

I stopped, my next words falling out of my mouth and evaporating like dew. *He loves me? How could he even say that after all this time?* I looked in the mirror, furiously searching, trying to see his face behind me, hoping to find the truth or the lie in it. *I thought he hated me.* I couldn't see him. I turned around to find him standing right behind me and I jumped, startled.

"Ghosts don't show up in mirrors," he whispered.

"I forgot."

We were silent for a minute. The air hung, sickly hot and sweet and tortuous, full of choices and opportunities. He slowly reached out and, for the first time, he touched me. Gently, his hand stroked my cheek and I could feel it. I gasped. *He can touch me.*

And in that moment, my defenses caved. My anger and confusion left me like tea seeping out of the bag and into the water. I stepped towards him and raised my hands to touch his face, which wasn't as cold as I had expected it to be. My heart seemed to stutter in my chest as I weighed my options. Before I could make a choice of my own, his head dipped down and his lips pressed against mine. *They aren't cold, either.* My hands nestled in his hair and, oh, how real it was. How real he was in my hands, in that moment. I pulled his hair, trying to drag his tall frame down to mine and relieve the gentle strain of my neck. He came down to me and I shivered from the feeling of his hands on my back, moving up and down, searching and feeling just as I was in his hair. I slowly ran my hands down his torso as our kiss deepened, feeling just how real he was, just how solid and alive he felt even without a beating heart or flowing blood.

He pulled away, seeming to remember that, while he didn't have to breathe, I did. He put his hands on top of mine, which were still on his chest. Only then did I realize the blue tint of his fingernails. I saw his blue-gray eyes searching my face and I wondered if they, too, had turned blue from the harsh reality of death, or if they were always that shade.

I can't believe we just did that. Should I still be mad? What does this mean for us? What does this mean for the band? What now?

Blades spoke, pulling me from my trance. "You know, I never doubted the band. I never doubted you." His words were so soft, they barely made it to my ears. "I think you're more than ready for this tour." His thumb rubbed gently against the back of my hand. "I was just worried about you guys. I know Mark told you about—" His voice caught in his throat. I searched his face as he had searched mine and I nodded.

"Blades?"

"Hm?"

"I love you too." We fell into another kiss, touching and feeling and grabbing and searching and all of it. We didn't hear the door open.

"Woah, Sam? Why are you making out with the air?" David asked.

Blades and I pulled apart and I could feel the blood rush to my face. Blades just smirked.

After a moment, something clicked in David's mind. "Wait a minute—hold on! Are you making out with one of the guys? Holy shit! How?! Why?! What?!"

Blades chuckled as I tried to speak. "I'm not sure how," I started. "And the 'why' is more personal." I felt the flush leave its home on my face, "Now, what did you want?"

David shook his head. "I was getting you for sound check."

"Sounds good. We *are* here to work, after all. We'll try to figure out this whole"—I gestured at Blades, not that David could see him—"situation after the show. Now, let's hop to it." I ushered David out of the room and turned back to smile at Blades, receiving one in reply.

"Wait a minute," I started, looking at him in whole. "Where are your feet?"

He stood in the middle of the room, but below his calves were gone, seeming to vanish into the floor.

"You pulled me down," he said. I raised an eyebrow at him. "It's simple, Sam. You're short and I'm tall, so I just had to get rid of my feet."

I burst into laughter and shook my head. "I love you," I repeated, and headed out to the stage.

<hr>

The lights went out on the stage and the crowd roared. The noise was excruciatingly loud—nothing coherent could be made out, it was just a wall of sound. Back behind the stage, we stood in a circle, hand in hand.

"Okay," I said, having to yell over the crowd, "tonight is our night. We're meant to be here. Everything we've done has brought us to this moment. So let's show everyone why we're here. Let's show them why we're the best." We threw our hands in the air as the voiceover came on the speakers.

"Ladies and gentlemen, are you ready?" Cheers. "The moment you've all been waiting for: welcome to the stage, Approaching Grace."

Amy, David, and Tom walked out on the stage to thunderous applause. They started playing a short instrumental piece we wrote to open the show. Cherie, my keyboard and mic tech, came over with my mic stand and mic as well as my ear monitors. I nodded at her and waited for my cue. I jumped from side to side and shook out my hands. *Okay, Sam. No more thinking about the hot ghost. Time to focus. You gave the pep talk, time to believe it.*

I ran out at my cue and was gladly received into the world of bright lights, loud sounds, and stifling heat. I threw my arms out to soak it all in and the crowd responded. Grinning, I popped my ear monitors in and faced the band, who ended the piece and immediately started our first song, the opener off our first album.

It was a beautiful night, not in terms of the weather or the place, but the people. As I ran and jumped and twirled onstage, the audience followed me. They sang along, screaming into the sky, cheering through the night. It flew by, song after song. Soon, too soon, we walked off the stage to cool off in our dressing rooms for a moment before our encore.

"Oh my God!" David exclaimed. "I can't believe this."

"They love us," Tom said, giddy.

I toweled myself dry, standing in their room. "I told y'all this would work," I said, patting my face lightly, trying not to remove my makeup. Blades appeared to me, smiling. I locked eyes with him and smiled back, nodding. "I told you."

Jason, our tour manager, walked towards us, "Hey guys. It's time."

I tossed my towel into the room, through Blades, with a smirk. "Let's go." *Just because I love him doesn't mean I forgive him entirely. He's getting there, though, and quickly.*

The cheering had continued while we were offstage. We walked on while the lights were down, but they saw us anyway. The cheers got louder as we got into position. The lights came up as wc hit the first chord of "Lights Up" by Stadium.

"Are you ready for this?" I asked the audience, and the

lights punched with the beat. As I sang, I ran back and forth on the stage, nodding my head side to side at the audience. When the guitar solo hit, I spun in a circle, jumping up and down, and as I did I caught the eyes of Stadium, standing side stage as we played their song. When I felt the warmth of their smiles, I stretched my arms out and spun again, soaking in everything—the audience, the brotherly love of the guys, the power of the band, all of it.

It felt like no time at all before the show was over. We locked hands center stage and threw our hands to the sky as we were flooded with sound. We ran backstage and to the guys' dressing room.

"That was insanity," Tom exclaimed.

"I can't believe we just did that," Amy said.

David didn't say anything; he just jumped up and down, screaming to himself. I laughed at him, grabbing him by the shoulders to settle him. He seemed to vibrate like a chihuahua and I couldn't help but shake my head at him. Our schedule was tight and we had to step to it in order to get to the next venue in time. We showered up quickly and headed back to the bus.

Invisible Touch

WE CLIMBED up the stairs of the bus, still shimmering with excitement from the show we'd just played.

"Evening, kids. Good show?" Mike asked.

"Hey Mike. It was awesome!" David exclaimed. The rest of us headed into the back of the bus while David held Mike captive in a conversation. I shook my head, smiling.

"What's so funny?" Blades said, apparating.

I ran at him, capturing him in a hug. The fading anger and excitement and love was overwhelming. I squeezed him tightly.

"Woah, woah, woah," Tom said.

"What the fuck?!" Amy exclaimed.

I buried my face in the crook of his neck, ignoring my two baffled friends. Everything melted away as I tried to commit him to memory. He was solid and strong, decorated in a variety of textures with his leather jacket conflicting with the soft fabric of his T-shirt and the rough metal of his belt buckle. He wasn't warm or cold, just there. He was totally silent, no heartbeat, no rising and falling chest, no small cough or sniffling nose—just desire without fire and love without heat. His hair brushed against my face with no smell. He was scentless in general. I brushed my hands over his face, feeling a light dusting of scruff—*he must not have shaved the day he died.*

As I came back to the present, I realized the eyes on us had increased. Now both bands stood around us, staring. David and Mark wore matching smirks while Tom and Amy still wore faces of bewilderment. I waved at our little crowd. "Hey guys."

"What the fuck?" Amy repeated. "Last time we talked, you were still pissed at him and, oh yeah—*you couldn't touch ghosts,*" she blurted out.

"I know, well, I don't know how, but—" I ran out of words. *How* is *this happening? Why is this happening? Is it because I died?*

"I might have a theory," Ronnie said. We all turned and looked at the usually silent bass player. The shadowy spirit seemed to shrink away from the attention for a moment, casting his eyes down before looking back up. "You know how we are visible on the bus? How we can touch the couches because they're ours? What if this is just the same concept?"

His words hung in the air as we breathed them in for consideration.

"What, so you own us now?" Amy asked.

"No, I think he's on to something," Mark started. "It's not that we own you, but that we know you. We're connected. Maybe."

"We never said we were ghost experts. This has never happened before," Ronnie added.

"So, can we all touch?" David asked, timidly.

"Only one way to find out," Mark said.

I held Blades' hand as we watched them. Hands reached towards hands with the fear of failure, or success. I felt my heart skip for a moment when Amy's fingers jammed into

Joey's. Mark and David, and Ronnie and Tom followed suit, each crashing like the one before. Laughter erupted in the cab and everyone broke into hugs.

"I never thought I'd feel this again," Mark said quietly, voice almost drowned in the loud room, but I heard him. As a short shiver ran down my spine, I pulled Blades back into my arms. *They haven't felt touch in decades. No one could feel them and they couldn't feel anyone. It was just them for years.*

"You will never be alone again," I said in Blades' ear, and he tightened his arms around me.

The weeks seemed to fly by as our bus rolled down the highway and, as they did, our album flew towards the top of the charts. The stage was our galaxy, our moon, and the audience—our stars, but the bus, our humble run-down bus, was our Earth, our grounding place of home. And in every home is a family.

And in every family, there's conflict.

"If this is what we can do alone, imagine what we could do with a label."

"David, you're not listening to what you're saying," Tom said. "If we're getting this far alone, why would we ever want to bring a label in? Right now, we're getting all the profit. Why would we want to give that up?"

"But, if we had a label, our potential earnings could go up and then our percentage would be higher than the total we have now," I proposed.

"Potentially, or we could get scammed into oblivion," Amy said.

We all broke into speaking once again, voices overlapping voices, reason trampling reason. We were sitting in the dining room, our space of business on the bus. It was late morning and we were waiting out our time before the next show by arguing. In the sidelines were Blades and Mark, who sat silently but watched with intent. Ronnie and Joey were in the back, still catching up on all the movies they had missed.

"We have it good right now. Things are great. Why do something we'd regret?" Tom said.

"We might *not* regret it. We just don't know. We should look into it at least," I replied. "Besides, have you ever considered that I might would enjoy some help running this business? That's what this band is—a business, and I have been running it alone for years now."

"Did you guys regret it?" David asked, turning the attention to Mark and Blades. Silence fell as the two looked at each other, seeming to talk without speaking. After a moment, Mark cleared his throat and spoke.

"I don't regret it. Kratter catapulted us to a global stage. It was amazing." David started to smile, smugly, in his seat, but I felt the sentence hang in the air. "But, that was in the eighties. We never could have gotten as far as you have without a label. You have a choice."

"I'm just saying we should do some research. Dip our toes in," I said, turning back to the guys and locking eyes with Amy.

"Sam, you've never been able to dip your toes into anything. You always jump in head first without checking the water for sharks," she replied, and I felt the bite in her words.

"Well, unlike you, I'm open to change and I'm not afraid of sharks," I heard myself say as a slap was painted on her face. Our words hung hot in the air, disturbing the quiet and making our bus feel more like a sauna than a home.

"Okay, let's cool it down," Mark said, stepping in between

all of us. I stood up and Blades put his hand on my shoulder before I stormed off to the living room.

"Hey, hey. What's up?" Joey asked, a hint of concern laced in his jovial voice.

I shook my head and sat down between him and Ronnie, turning my attention to the TV where they were watching *Flubber*. I sighed with a small smile. "Never change, guys."

The hours crawled by. It was only two o'clock when the movie ended. Everyone had trickled into the living room, leading to a slight tension in the air. But, laugh by laugh, joke by joke, we fell into a timid comfort, a light easiness that lingered after the screen went dark. We sat around in the silence for a moment.

"You know, I think that regret is a useless emotion," Mark said, breaking the silence.

My eyes drifted from the black screen to our carpeted flooring, making note of how it absorbed and displayed our individual footprints when we walked into the room. Four sets of footprints for eight people. *Even more proof of the lie we live.*

"You asked if we regret our record contract and I don't. But I sometimes regret it because it led to me treating Chrissie so shitty."

"Chrissie?" Amy questioned.

"My wife."

"You were married?" I asked. "I never saw anything about you being married and I used to run a Stadium fan club."

"Well, that was by design," he said. He settled into the couch, almost as if he were attempting to bury himself into the cushions. He stared down at his hand and pulled a ring off of his right middle finger before sliding it onto his left ring finger. "The idea was to make it seem like I was single to hook in the girls." He huffed a sigh through a slight, sad smile. "And it worked. Too well."

"And what about Chrissie?" Amy whispered.

Mark shook his head. "I never told her, but she knew."

"How do *you* know?" she pressed.

The air was thick to the point where it was almost hard to breathe. The grief in the atmosphere seemed to choke him as he spoke, "Well, Chrissie always had a, uh, addictive personality. So, she—"

Blades reached out and put his hand on Mark's shoulder, stopping him. He whispered something to him and Mark nodded.

Mark cleared his throat, as if he were going to speak, but he stopped. I tried to think of something to say, some sort of reassuring platitude, but my words ran out. My breath left me like a death rattle and no one seemed to move, breath, or blink.

Out of the abyss, Joey blurted out, "I miss my mom."

Like a splash of paint on a blank canvas or a stab in the heart, the feeling of anguish struck me like nothing else.

"You've always been a momma's boy," Blades said, tenderly.

Joey nodded. "I never told her goodbye. And she must have been so scared when she heard—" His words blanked out. His mouth stood agape for a moment before he shook his hair, forking his fingers in it, and finally revealing a curtain he built between him and us. "I would call her every night before the show and that night, I ran out of time. I didn't tell her I loved her."

"She knew," I said, and offered my hand to Joey to hold.

"But I didn't tell her. I should've called her. I could've been late. Postponed the show a few minutes. I should've called her." He swatted my hand away gently.

"You didn't know. You couldn't have known," David assured.

"I knew."

The whole group turned to face Ronnie, who showcased a frown.

"How?" Tom asked.

Ronnie shrugged. "I had a bad feeling. I didn't know that it'd happen *that day* and all. But I knew." I watched as his eyes locked with Blades' and Blades seemed to crumble under his gaze. "I tried to get the label to push it off, to give us a break so we could recover. We had *just* gone on a tour. But no. We *had* to go on another tour. Fuckin' corporate hack jobs got us killed."

"It wasn't the company," Blades started.

"Hey, no—" Mark interjected.

"No, it's my fault."

"They pushed you to do it," Joey said.

Blades jumped up and stood in the middle of the room. "No. I talked to the label and told them we should tour because of the album. It's all *my* fault. It's me." I stood to go to him, but he held up his hand to me. "It's my fault we're trapped here."

"I don't blame you," Ronnie said with a sigh.

The guys stood and surrounded him with a hug. It was a long moment before anyone spoke, but eventually Blades spoke up.

"You know, we four are stuck together forever." He sniffed like he was going to cry, but there were no tears for the spirit. "We fought. Hell, we fought a fuck-ton, let's be honest. But, being dead puts it all in perspective." He looked at us, locking eyes with each of us. "This seems like a big deal now, but it doesn't matter. Nothing matters—just the connections, the people you have are worth more than any argument, than being right." The ghosts nodded their heads vigorously.

I felt my eyes meet Amy's. She gave a soft smile. "I'm sorry," I said.

"I'm sorry too." We hugged, holding each other tight to brace against the trembling of the bus. David and Tom joined us as we stood, a solid bundle of arms and warmth, hugging in the middle of the living room.

"Wow, Blades. When did you become a philosopher?" Ronnie asked.

"Same time you became a gynecologist," he replied, and everyone broke into laughter.

I'll never forget the show that night. I'm not going to get into it here—some things should remain sacred—and I think that writing it down will diminish it. Let's just say that that night in Austin, Texas, was one of the best nights of my life, not just as a performer, but as a person. That was the last time I truly felt on top of the world. Free.

Life in the Fast Lane

Our headlining tour was in full swing when I got the call. We were somewhere in the Southwest, just barely free of the chill of winter that had settled over most of the country. We were in the middle of soundcheck and I almost didn't pick up the phone.

My phone wouldn't stop vibrating in my pocket. Taking my left hand off the keyboard, I reached into my pocket to fish it out. Around me, people were checking cables, adjusting lights, and setting up chairs. My vocals reverberated around the room as I looked at my phone. *No name. Probably spam. But, maybe not...* In my gut, I felt the need to answer it. *Maybe something awful has happened...* I shook my head at myself, but raised my hands anyway, stopping the band.

"Sorry—phone call." I answered the phone.

"Come on—" David started. I held up my finger, shushing him.

As the caller spoke, my hand shook. My finger fell from

David's mouth and down to my side as my mouth dropped open. The caller stopped speaking and I struggled to regain my voice. "Uh yes, yes. We'll be there. Please send all of the information to this number and we'll be there. Thank you."

The call was over. I stood there, still, glued to the middle of the stage.

"What's wrong, Sam?" Tom asked.

"Yeah, who died?" David asked, only half-joking.

I shook my head slowly before the words finally fell out. "We're up for a Grammy." The guys looked at me and shock painted their faces.

Our assistant tour manager, Joan, smiled at us from the stage wings. She cupped her hands around her mouth. "Attention everyone. Approaching Grace is now a Grammy-nominated band!"

All around us, the crew started clapping, one by one people joined in till everyone was cheering, stomping, and whooping. The four of us came together in the middle of the stage and hugged. We were doing it. Now it's real.

"So what are we going to wear to the ceremony?" Amy asked. The question hung heavy in the center of the living room.

"We could get a stylist—custom suits and shit. We'd be just like real celebrities!" David said. His excitement exploded into the air, seeming to cover us all in the glitter of his energy.

I sat up in my seat on the couch. "Custom outfits are likely out of the question, David." I watched him start to steel his resolve, so I continued. "Yes, we've got some money and we're wearing big famous-people pants now, but we still have monetary obligations. Do you want to tell the crew that we're docking their pay because we wanted to look famous?" I said, gently.

David buried himself into a blanket mound next to Tom. Only his mouth was visible when he said, "I guess not."

Tom chucked at him, lightly, and patted his blanketed head. "Yeah, we're gonna have to go naked to save for gas money." Amy barked out a laugh as David finally hid his whole body in the mountain.

"No, not quite. We're not a Twinkie away from collapse or anything," I said, smiling.

"You guys might want some guidance on this, though," Mark chimed in. "I remember the awards shows when we were alive were brutal on fashion. Of course, we aimed for the laid-back, no-shits-given look, but it was still rough."

"Well, it's funny that you say that, Mark. I was actually going to suggest that we meet with a stylist to put together outfits—not from scratch, but like, go shopping for us. Make sure we fit in with the crowd, but stand out at the same time," I said.

Blankets went flying as limbs shot out of the mountain, "Really?!"

"Yes, really."

David jumped out of his seat, "Hell yeah!"

I grabbed him by the hand, "Come on, let's start researching some stylists." And like a parent with their child at the mall, I led David to the front of the bus to grab our laptops and get to work.

The days leading up to the Grammys were full of shows and planning for the awards ceremony, so time seemed to fly by. The night was upon us and it threatened to fly by in a blur of red velvet, bright lights, and sparkles. When we stepped out of our rented limo, we were immediately met by a guide, a man in a brilliant white suit. Our white knight shepherded us down the red carpet and in front of a horde of photographers.

"Approaching Grace," the suited man announced. With that, the mob was unleashed on us. Like an atomic bomb going off, we were suddenly bathed in light. I was so startled, I flinched. But that was nothing. It was then that the yelling began.

"Ms. Roland, give us a smile."

"Come on, huddle up now."

"Act like you want to be here, guys."

"Relax!"

"Come on!"

We fell in line. Like the newbies we were, we had practiced poses in front of the mirror beforehand, trying to find the best shots for our heights, outfits, and positions in the band. We eventually settled on one and practiced it until it became second nature. Now, it seemed that training was going to pay off.

Tom and David framed us, looking tall and in control in their similar suits. Tom wore a more traditional, black suit with a silky white shirt. He had no tie; instead, a large blue necklace was visible in the gap of his unbuttoned shirt. David mirrored him in a black, glittery suit with a light blue shirt and a collection of necklaces. Next to David was Amy. Her brown hair was teased up and she had blue eyeshadow that matched the blue silk blouse she wore over black bell-bottoms. I was between her and Tom, in a light blue crop top and a black miniskirt. I was wearing layered belts, silver bangle bracelets, and bejeweled tights. We were shiny, blue, and matching, but we were individual and different at the same time—just what we had wanted.

Our white-suited leader soon ushered us along, away from the flashing cameras and raised voices. We were led into the theater and passed along to another man to be taken to our seats.

The room was filled with rows and rows of seats towards the back of the room, but as we moved closer to the stage, the rows were replaced with large, circular tables. We arrived at a table with our name on a white card.

"Sort of a schmancy set up, here," David joked, but his voice was soft, breathless. Across the table was another table card marked Halestorm.

"Do you think we really have a chance?" Tom whispered.

"We're here, aren't we?" I replied.

The room slowly began to fill with people as the time for the ceremony crept closer. Famous faces were everywhere. Soon, the overhead lights dimmed and the show began.

"And the Grammy for Best New Artist goes to..." The announcer made a show of opening the envelope. Two screens were positioned on the sides of the stage. Four video feeds were being played—three other artists and us. Our hands were clasped together in the center of the table as we awaited the results. Blades was next to me, his hands on my shoulders.

"Remember, it doesn't matter if you win. Either way, you still get the acknowledgement and the status of having been nominated," he said. As usual, no one around us could see him, so I simply nodded once before turning my focus back to the announcer.

She finally opened the envelope and, with a big smile, she said, "Approaching Grace!"

David was the first of us to jump up. "Oh my God!" He grabbed Tom's hand and pulled him out of his seat. Amy and I got up and went after him towards the stage. When we got on the stage, the announcer handed the award to Amy.

"I can't believe we're actually here right now, never mind the fact that we actually won," Amy said. The crowd chuckled lightly. "I want to thank my Mom and Dad and my three best friends here for making this crazy dream work. Thank you."

"This one's for you, Mamá!" David said after her.

Tom walked up next. "Thank you, Dad. And thanks to all of our friends."

Then it was time for me. "I want to thank all of our parents and friends. I also want to thank our amazing fans for getting us here today. We love you and we will see you out on the road." I hesitated for a moment. *Time is running out. Either say it or wrap it up, Roland.* "And thanks to Blades, Mark, Ronnie, and Joey." Amy cut her eyes back at me, shock and fear on her face. "Thanks guys, wherever you are."

We walked off the stage and back to our seats. The eyes began to leave us as the next category was introduced and the world carried on with its rotation. Once we sat down, Amy tore into me.

"Sam!" she hissed, "Why did you say that? People could find out."

"Do you really think anyone is going to put those names together and immediately assume that we talk to ghosts?" My voice held a laugh in it, not yet expressed. "Besides, every one of our fans knows that we're Stadium fans. It was vague enough. We'll be fine."

She shuddered out a sigh. "That still was risky. Imagine if you ever told anyone you, and the rest of us, could see ghosts?"

"The government could take us all away," David whispered, joining the conversation suddenly.

"We're not mermaids, David," Tom scoffed.

"Yeah, but they've done worse for less—"

"David, can we get into your conspiracy theories when we aren't in the middle of an awards ceremony?" Amy said. "We just have to finish things up here, do any exit interviews, and then get back to the limo. Then everything will be back to normal." She settled back into her seat, seeming to relax.

I raised my glass from the table and directed towards my bandmates. "Cheers?" I offered.

Three glasses clinked against mine. As I sipped my drink, the four apparitions appeared before me and smiled. I gestured my drink towards them as well, nodding in appreciation. *This one's for you.*

This Is Not a Test

Between our chart success and Grammy win, it wasn't all that surprising when our talks of joining a record label suddenly took a real turn. Our success meant that instead of having to seek one out, one approached us. In the early 2010s, the time of YouTube and SoundCloud, it was pretty unusual for labels to go after bands. Gone were the days of label reps scoping out dive bars for talent. Despite this, that is exactly what happened. We were still pretty surprised when it happened, it was so unexpected. Perhaps the oddity of the situation should have been a clue, but we were still young and, as always, hindsight is twenty-twenty.

The lights dimmed to black as the show at the Fletcher County Performing Arts Center came to a close. The crowd was amazing, displaying the growing trend of people singing along to our original songs during the shows. We walked off the stage and into the small side stage area where the sound guy sat. Scurrying past him, we headed down a narrow, brightly lit hallway with walls decked out in signatures of the bands who had previously played there and posters of all shapes and sizes. As we headed towards the dressing rooms, which were situated at the end of the hall, I ran to David, my boots squeaking against the white tile floor.

"God, could they have been more into it? That was great. That was great!" David smiled at my display of post-concert-adrenaline before I peeled myself off of him and jogged towards the front of our little crowd. "Tom! Tell me that wasn't damn near perfect. Go ahead, tell me!" He smirked and I was gone again. I ran back towards Amy, hopping like the Energizer Bunny. "How do you feel? Wasn't it awesome?" Amy's smile was weak, but present—clearly exhausted by the show instead of energized like myself. Before she could speak, another voice joined the conversation.

"I, for one, thought it was."

The backstage was outfitted with a few small meeting rooms on each side of the hallway before you reached the dressing rooms. The voice came from one of them and, as if in a horror movie, our little detail changed course to follow the sound. In the room sat an older man in a gray suit with a skinny blue tie.

When we entered, he stood up from the circular table in the middle of the room and offered his hand to Tom with a grin. "I've been following you guys for a while and, I just have to say, you are one of the best groups I've seen in a long time. And that's saying a lot 'cause I've been around for an even longer time."

The dull light in the room shined off of the man's partially bald head, though the short distance between his head and the ceiling meant that the reflection didn't go very far. He shook Tom's hand before moving down the line to each member, saying each of our names with a broad smile. He finally reached me.

"Samantha Roland. So nice to finally meet you. I know I'm not the first to say it, but you are bound to be the biggest female rock singer of your generation. You're going to take Evanescence and Paramore and send them running for the hills!"

His hand held mine in a tight grip without faltering. My mouth fell open for a second before I was able to regain control of myself. "Thank you, Mr....?"

"Oh, of course. Forgive me. I'm just so excited to meet you that I've forgotten myself. I am Jim Kratter, of Kratter Records. I've come to talk to you about an interesting proposition."

Kratter Records...that's the label that signed Stadium!

"How did you get in here?" David blurted.

"Oh, I'm a friend of the manager here. I told him that I wanted to talk to you, if you'll allow me." He gestured to the seats around a small oval wooden table in the middle of the meeting room.

We sat down to listen to what Mr. Kratter had to say.

"Thank you for taking this time to listen to me. I know you're very busy." He smiled again. "Now, the reason I'm here is that I want to offer you the opportunity to record on my label."

Are you shitting me?

"You guys are doing pretty well on your own right now." He hesitated, looking as if he was worried we'd be mad at his next words, yet he continued. "But I've seen your numbers and I think you could greatly benefit from my label's services. We have a top-of-the-line promotional team, some of the best sound engineers you could hope for, and a long history of signing multi-platinum selling artists."

This is too good to be true.

His hands moved the entire time that he was talking, as if he was trying to swat away some unseen bug. He continued on his sell. "We even have the privilege of being able to say that we were the label for the late, great eighties hair band Stadium before their tragic demise."

"That's where I've heard your name before," Tom said softly.

Kratter showed a shark's smile and carried on. "Yep! Stadium was one of our biggest bands." He began to twist the ring on his left pinky finger. "They were a great *asset* to our label...great people too, of course. I understand they're a big influence for you."

"More than you'd know," David blurted, again. I kicked him softly under the table before grabbing the conversation again.

"Yeah, they inspire us a lot."

"Well, then I hope this offer doesn't fall on deaf ears. We would love to welcome you on as a new act on the label. We were thinking of a two-album contract, with a good amount of advances and percentages for all your hard work. Here"— Kratter slid a thick stack of papers across the table to me— "take a look at this contract and, once you've made up your mind, you can either mail it back to me with your signatures or sign the last page with the decline on it."

Kratter stood up and we stumbled to do the same.

This is insane.

"Thank you, Mr. Kratter. We'll definitely talk this out and get back to you as soon as we can," I said, extending my hand for him to shake.

"Great. I'd like to hear from you by the end of the month. We have to be efficient with these things, you see," he said, shaking my hand.

"I understand. You'll hear from us."

"Perfect. Have a nice night." He walked out of the room and we let out a collective breath.

"This is great! This is exactly what we've been talking about!"

"David, calm down, he's likely still in the hallway. We can't show our cards at any point in this," Amy said. "Besides, I don't know. He gives me a bad vibe."

"I'm not so sure, Ams—he seems pretty legit. And he worked with the guys. But, either way, we should get that contract to a lawyer before anything else," Tom said, and made a move for the door.

"Good points all around. I'm not sure how I feel about all of this yet, so let's set about that first thing in the morning," I said. We walked back out into the hallway and towards the dressing rooms. "This has been more than enough excitement for one night, I think. Let's shower up and head to the bus. And step on it, because he took up a good amount of our time with his proposal already."

"You got it, boss," David said, and I rolled my eyes.

The bus rocked lightly as we got on.

"Have a good show guys?" Mike asked.

"Always, Mike. Always," I said.

"Good, good."

We walked past him and threw ourselves around the cabin. The contract felt heavy in my hands, and truly, it was. It must have been over a hundred pages, at least. As the bus pulled from the parking lot, Mark appeared to us.

"I heard everything in the meeting. This is great!"

"I know, right? This could be our big moment!" David said.

Amy grabbed the TV remote and clicked it on. "I'm not so sure, guys. A two-album contract, all those benefits... It seems too good. Let's not count our chickens before they hatch. We need to wait till we hear back from a lawyer."

"That's fair," Mark said. "We jumped into our contract with them blind. It wasn't the smartest move, but nothing bad happened."

"Well—you *did* die," David harped, and Mark rolled his eyes and gestured vaguely at the stack of paper in front of me, smoke wisping around.

"Whatever, man. It's not like the contract did it or anything." The two of them were snickering, but I was staring at Amy. *I get her hesitance, but she could at least be happy about it. I don't understand why this has been such a big issue with her.*

———

In the time after this, things were tense, to say the least. Tom's lawyer uncle looked at the contract and gave it the green light, so it was now the situation of deciding whether or not we would actually sign on with Kratter. Our arguments regarding whether or not to join with a label at all continued, with talks about limousines and Ritz-Carlton hotels being countered with thoughts of artistic freedom and higher profit margins. Throughout the whole thing, Amy's initial apprehension didn't go away. If anything, it got worse.

———

"This whole situation just rubs me the wrong way. I mean, who approaches bands at shows anymore? How did he even find out about us?"

"Amy, we were signed to that same label and it was good. They were good guys and I mean, hey, they got us as far as we got," Blades said, sitting down on the couch next to me, his cloud puffing up into the air when he hit the couch. He put his arm around me and I smiled at his touch.

"Plus, we're an Emmy-award-winning band. We're not nobodies anymore," I pitched.

"But how is this company still around? Their Wiki said that they haven't even been that active since the nineties. Why are they back all of a sudden? Isn't that weird to you?" She ran her hands through her hair in distress.

"Ams—the contract is good and Mr. Kratter seemed really nice. I get why you were suspicious, but it all checks out. Let's at least go check out the place. We could talk to him again and you could ask him questions, if that would make you more comfortable," I said.

"Well, it sounds like you've already made your mind up, then." Amy twisted away from us on the couch across from ours, not making eye contact.

"All I'm saying is that we have two weeks before he wants the contract back, acceptance or denial. We should at least do all of our research before we just throw this opportunity away on one of your hunches—" I barely finished talking before she was out of the room, murmuring something about "hunches" and headed to the back of the bus where David and Joey were watching a movie. I sighed and looked at the ground for a moment. The swirling red shapes on the black carpet reminded me of an arcade.

"Come on Phil, let's go play the claw games!" I called out, running after Amy to the building's entrance.

"No, Stevie Ray! You know they give me a bad feeling. Those things are rigged." She pulled open the door and we entered the darkened room, filled with flashing lights and a glowing, swirling carpet. "Let's go play skee ball. I'm really good at it."

"Okay." We ran to the back of the building, where the machines were.

"And later we can get pizza!"

"Yeah!"

"Hey, Mork calling Orson. Come in, Orson." His reference made me come out of my memory and back to the present. I grabbed the hand that Blades had lazily draped on my shoulder and made long strokes on it with my thumb.

I shook my head, in spite of myself. "I just don't know what to do, Blades. I don't know why she is so against this for us. She won't tell me why. It's always just 'I have a bad feeling.'" I shifted in my seat on the couch and I felt his arm tighten around me. "She's always been like this. Obsessed with her hunches and bad feelings. Want to know what else she had a bad feeling on? Me taking the alternate route home after school one day. I did what she said and took the normal route and then boom—car accident."

"You probably shouldn't be judging her off a mistake she made years ago—"

"My car got totaled." I looked at our gray ceiling. "I still miss it."

"Even so—" He moved his arm from my shoulder to talk with his hands, as he was prone to do when he wanted to make a point or think out a tough situation. "Don't put her down completely. She made some good points when you were talking before." I grabbed his floating hands and held them in my own.

"Her arguments have been solid, but nothing that I haven't been able to counter with my own, valid points. She won't even look into the details without going on about her odd feelings and half-made points." An idea bubbled into my head. " I think that I'm going to go talk to Mr. Kratter again tomorrow at his office. Maybe I can get some information that'll change her mind." I looked at how the gray seemed to encroach upon the blue in his eyes and I felt that pit in the bottom of my stomach again. "I won't do this without her. I can't."

Blades nodded, solemnly. "If you think that's the best idea, then I support you." He settled back down into the couch, relaxing from his ranting pose and letting the cushions swallow him. "I was always fighting with Mark. I was convinced that I didn't need him. Even after we died, we were still fighting, always at each other's throats, fighting about whose fault it was that we're stuck here." He went quiet for a while, staring off in the distance. When his mind returned back to him, he smiled at me. "I think we're about to pull up in San Diego."

"Welcome to San Diego, guys," Mike called from the front.

"How did you know that? Could you, like, perceive that we were entering a new area or—" Blades started laughing. "What, what?"

"No—I just saw the road sign."

"Oh," I said, and dropped my head into my palm. He smiled at me again, that full, radiant smile in spite of everything,

"Don't worry. I'm confused about what I can do a lot of the time too." At that, we both laughed and I began to plan what I'd say to Mr. Kratter when I saw him the next day.

My visit with Mr. Kratter was very short. He just barely fit me in in between meetings and, once in, I had to be quick so that I could get back to the venue for the night's show. Despite this, I felt that I had done a good job of collecting information for Amy. I returned to the venue to little fanfare. It seemed that no one had noticed that I was gone.

I went down the central hallway to find the dressing room that I was sharing with Amy. This was a newer venue, so the backstage was roomier than most, allowing us to split up from our usual four-person unit. When I got to the room, Amy was putting on makeup in front of a lighted vanity. As I sat my bag down on the table behind her, she spoke.

"Where've you been?"

I watched as she curved her mouth into a perfect "o" shape to put on her eyeliner, and smiled.

"I decided to swing by Kratter's office to see if I could get some more information about the label and—"

"You did what?" The smile that I wore was now gone as I looked at her, her eyes boring a hole into me through the mirror. "What did you do, Sam?"

"I just asked him to tell me more about the past acts that have worked for him and why he was interested in us and we agreed to set up a trial period with the label so we could test it out and see—"

"I can't believe you. I really can't." She stood up and began to shove her makeup supplies into her bag. "You went there, without telling anyone, and started making goody-goody with the fucking president of the label. I can't believe this." She moved away from the vanity and towards the door. "Just how much did you sell our souls for, Samantha?" Not waiting for me to respond, she went out the door, slamming it.

"Oh my God." I stared at the reflection of the door in the mirror and didn't move. *What just happened?*

If it wasn't clear that Amy was mad at me, I could definitely tell during the show. Every song was too fast, with too many drum fills, throwing me off rhythm more than once and straining my voice as I sang. And no matter how many times I tried to signal for her to slow down or threw a pleading look her way, she wouldn't give—marching us on to the end of the show as if we were being chased. We almost ended early, with how fast she was going, but I stalled just enough to make up for it.

When we went to do our final bows, Amy stood at the end

of our line instead of next to me as she always did. Walking off the stage felt just as solitary, noticing that, all of a sudden, I was alone on stage, my bandmates having run off to the back-stage area as if the place was on fire.

The backstage was silent aside from the sounds of showers running. I got in a shower as Amy was coming out. She walked by me as if she had never seen me in her life, like she couldn't see me at all. The shower that followed felt cold, despite the obvious steam that was coming off the water.

The bus was just as quiet. When Mike asked how the show was, I could only shrug. He, perhaps noticing the look on my face, only nodded slowly before turning back to look at the book he had been reading. Instead of hanging out with each other like normal, we all retired to our bunks without a word. Whether the boys were mad at me or not, I didn't know. It was possible that Amy had already told everyone what I had done. Maybe she was waiting to tear me apart in front of them. But all I knew was that, whenever I closed my eyes, the only thing I could picture was Amy's cold eyes looking through me.

Eruption

THE NEXT MORNING WAS HOT. We were in Phoenix, Arizona, and at just ten a.m., it was 97 degrees. It was projected to reach a scorching 106 degrees by 2 p.m.

I can't believe I booked Arizona in July. I shook my head and turned my phone off. A bit of light crept in around the edges of my curtain but it was quickly snuffed out by the suffocating darkness of my bunk. In the distance, voices mixed with the sounds of the radio and the TVs. In the middle of it all, I could hear Amy laughing.

"I can't do this," I mumbled.

"Why not?" A voice crept in. *Blades.* He wasn't here; just his voice peeked out of that realm that he sometimes called home.

I sighed and rolled over, turning my back to the curtain. I pulled my blanket up over my ear. "I can't do it."

I woke up an hour later when the bus flew forward in a lurch. "What the fuck?" I crawled out of my bunk and braced myself, putting a hand on each side of the bunk hall. I looked forward into the dining room and saw David, Tom, and Amy each still bracing against the couch, the table, and the fridge, clearly frazzled.

"Gotdamn!" Mike shouted from the front.

"What happened?" Amy asked.

I saw Mike gesture, pointedly, at the road, "Some jackass cut us off so tight, I had to pull off and slam on the brakes to avoid hitting him."

"Yeah, I felt that part," David muttered.

"Are you okay?" I called up. "Is *everyone* okay?"

"Bus is all right, I'm all right," Mike replied.

"Are you guys good?" I asked again, plodding softly into the vast field of uncertainty, waiting for a shot to the abdomen to drop me on the ground.

Amy let go of the table and moved to sit at it instead. David sat on the couch.

"We're okay," Tom said softly, his eyes pleading my allegiance to his vow of nonintervention.

"Okay, good." I backed up, back down the hallway. "I'm going to brush my teeth." I grabbed my toothpaste out of the medicine cabinet and closed the mirror. Sighing, I drew a line of toothpaste on my toothbrush. As I went to put the brush in my mouth, someone grabbed my arm.

"Sam, I—"

"Jesus Christ!" The toothbrush flew out of my hand before I realized that it was Blades who had touched me. He frowned as the brush fell through his visage and onto the floor. I bent down to grab it, wiping up the toothpaste that was now also on the ground. "You need to announce yourself next time."

"I keep forgetting. I'm sorry."

I reapplied the toothpaste and got on with brushing my teeth. "What do you want?" I said, my voice garbled.

"I wanted to offer a piece of advice. For dealing with Amy."

I closed the bathroom door, forcing us closer together and, hopefully, muffling the sound of Blades' low, rumbling voice. *If she hears this, she might think we're going behind her back... again.* I gestured for him to continue.

"Whenever Mark and I used to fight, and I actually felt like trying to make it up to him, I would get him a gift. Something small, but something that reminded him of our friendship." Blades shrugged. "It worked most of the time. Though, if it was a really big argument, I'd just buy him some blow."

I spat out my toothpaste and shook my head. "And you wonder why you're dead." I rinsed the sink and prepared to head back into the bus. "I can't buy her blow, but I could probably do the first thing."

A few hours passed on the bus before we got to our final destination of the day. The Skyline Arena was huge—easily one of the biggest places we had played all tour. And luckily, it was a closed arena, so the stifling heat would not be able to reach us during the show. At least, the heat of the weather. The heat of Amy's gaze was a different story. But, I was prepared. Before sound check, I ran out to accomplish my task. *Blades better be right about this.*

Amy and I had had very few fights in our entire friendship —that was part of why we were so close. Most of our fights were little, trivial things—arguments over songs and setlist orders—nothing this big. The protocol was shaky, unfirm. But, I looked at my apology gift in my hands and nodded. *This will do...hopefully.*

I laid the gift down on my makeup table and looked around the room. We each had our own dressing rooms, part of the glamour of being the headliner at some venues. After being in a cramped tour bus for so long, it was nice to be alone in some respects. And with the tensions of the morning, some alone time was very refreshing.

Of course, I haven't been entirely alone in years....

"I see you're taking Blades' advice," Mark said, appearing in the room.

"Well, what else am I supposed to do?" I went over to my road case and unpacked my electric tea kettle.

"You could apologize," he offered, sitting down on the armchair next to me.

I kept at my task, setting up the kettle on the counter, plugging it into a socket gingerly. "You know I've tried. She cut me off." I went back to my case and grabbed a bottle of water to put in the kettle. I turned it on and waited.

"But did you? Did you really apologize?" He paused and I tried to review my conversation with Amy, but I could only hear her yelling at me. Mark continued. "For someone as fearless as you, I'm shocked to see you be such a coward."

"What?" I turned around slowly and looked at him.

"You heard me." There was no malice on Mark's face, only a soft smile.

"I'm scared of hurting Amy."

"No you're not."

"How are you going to tell me how I feel? You're not in my head."

"No, but I've been in your shoes." He stood up and walked over to the counter, putting his back to the kettle. "When Blades and I used to fight, I wasn't worried about him. I was worried about two things: the band and myself."

"But Amy and I *don't* fight. You and Blades were at each other's throats ninety percent of the time over everything and anything. You knew what he'd do in these situations, how he'd react. I don't know about Amy."

"You're just proving my point, Sam." He grabbed me by the shoulder, a move straight from my dad's handbook, and dropped his head, finding my eyes where they lingered on his shirt. "You're not afraid of hurting Amy. You are afraid of getting hurt."

The kettle started to scream in front of me and, for a moment, neither of us moved. Mark's kind, earnest eyes bore into my own. I broke away and turned off the kettle, then filled one of my mugs with the steaming water. I dropped in a tea bag. "And maybe I am. What's wrong with that?" I whispered.

"Nothing, as long as you don't let it get in the way of your fixing things."

I nodded as I bobbed my tea bag, watching it seep into the water.

"You're all living the dream right now. Don't be the one who wakes up."

I looked up at Mark. "You're right." Picking up the gift, I moved towards the door. Mark gave me a curt nod, which I returned as he vanished out of sight.

Amy's room was across the hall from mine. *Don't let the dream die,* I thought, and knocked.

After a brief infinity, the door opened. Amy was halfway through getting dressed, wearing a sparkly blouse with a pair of sweatpants. Her hair was up in curlers and her makeup was done.

"What?" Her voice was clipped, short and stern.

"Oh, I'm sorry. I don't want to interrupt anything."

"You already have." She sighed. Opening the door wider, she gestured for me to come in. I walked in behind her and sat down on the couch. Amy sat down opposite of me in front of a drum pad. She grabbed the finger tape that she used to protect her hands and started to wrap her fingers. "So, why are you here?"

"I think you might know," I said, somewhat sheepishly.

"You've come to apologize?" I nodded and she returned it. "Okay. Go on then."

I shifted on the couch and cleared my throat, "Okay. Amy. I am sorry, deeply, truly sorry. I know that I went behind your back, but that wasn't my intention. I was just trying to research the label so we could discuss it with all the details."

"'Researching' doesn't require you making a deal, Sam." She stood up and put back the finger tape, slamming the drawer of the road case closed. "You could've just talked to them and come back."

"And that was my intention, but Kratter laid out the deal and it was so perfect, what with the trial period and—"

"Oh come on, Sam! You know that was too good to be true! Labels lie all the time. It was a trap."

"You don't know that. You didn't hear Kratter, he—"

"Yeah, you're right. I didn't hear him. Want to know why? Because you didn't include me. You went by yourself. You told no one and then you made a decision on behalf of the whole band by yourself. You included no one, not even me."

Silence filled the room, a stiff, stifling, oppressive, ugly thing. *There it is.* In all of our years of friendship, we'd bickered and groaned, pissed each other off, and been just plain mad, but this was new territory. I stared down at my lap, at the gift I still held in my hands.

There was a knock at the door. "Hey guys. On stage in five."

"Thanks, Jason," Amy called.

I stood up slowly. "I have more to say on this, but I have to finish getting ready." I walked over to her, avoiding her eyes, and placed the wrapped gift on the table. "I'll see you side stage." I left the room and crossed the hall. When I closed the door behind me, Blades was there.

"How did it go?"

I let out a shaky sigh and he came over to me, wrapping his arms around me, tight.

"That bad?"

"It wasn't awful, but I really don't know." His hand nestled in my hair and I nuzzled into the touch. "We're not done talking. She hasn't opened the picture yet, but I apologized."

He held me at an arm's length for a moment, his gray-blue eyes locking onto mine. "Well," he started, his voice soft, yet firm, "you did all you could. It's just up to Amy now."

But did I? I folded myself back into his embrace. "You're right." I pulled away and double-checked my hair and makeup in the mirror. His reflection was missing from the reflection, as always. I sighed and grabbed my tea mug, now slightly cooler than it was before.

There was a knock on the door. "Time to go," Jason called.

I started towards the door and Blades grabbed my arm.

"Hey, knock 'em dead."

I smiled softly and nodded before leaving the room and heading down the halls to the stage. *What will Amy say to me? Will she speak to me at all? Did she open the gift?* I tried to calm my thoughts, instead shifting my focus to the sound of the crowd outside. Their voices echoed down into the halls and seemed to grow as I got closer. I shook out my limbs, passing my tea mug from hand to hand to avoid spilling it. When I got to side stage, I handed it to Cherie to put on the stage. As she did that, a newer roadie Todd, got me set up with my in-ear monitors. David and Tom met me and also started to get set up. I tossed a smile at them, which Tom returned, but David did not.

"We seriously need to talk later," David said.

"Okay. We can talk on the bus," I replied, and he nodded.

"Did you talk to Amy?" Tom asked.

"Yeah, I did." I clipped my wireless microphone pack onto the waistband of my pants. "We didn't get too far into it, but—"

I was interrupted by the sound of stomping boots.

"What the hell is this?" Amy stood face to face with me, and David and Tom quickly split to the sides of us, creating walls to contain any potential explosion. In one set of wrapped fingers, she held her drumsticks, and in the other she held a picture frame. It was a plain frame, black coating on wood, but the contents were the shining light. Within the simple frame was a photo of Amy and me, aged twelve, at our middle school talent show. Amy's hair was in pigtails and my bangs were clipped back. Our clothes were tacky and we looked entirely too dorky for the rock show we were trying to put on at the time, but we were cute and full of joy and love, neither of which were present on Amy's face now.

"What is this, Samantha?" Angie, Amy's drum tech, came up behind her and started to wire her up.

"It's an apology present. I wanted to get something to remind you of us, of our friendship." I moved to touch her shoulder, but she dodged me. "We've been friends for so long, I just wanted to call attention to that, I guess." My voice dwindled as Amy continued to stare me down.

"All these years of friendship, you go behind my back, and then give me a picture." She hit the word like a ball with a bat. She shook her head, disgusted. "I guess I never knew you at all."

The music on stage changed to our walk-on cue as the lights went out. Amy's eyes were locked on mine, cold and hard as steel. Tom and David went out on the stage. Amy turned on her heel and followed closely behind. My feet were stuck to the floor as shock began to drip out of my pores. An unseen hand pressed against my back, shoving me on the stage. I turned back as I began my trek and saw Mark and Blades in the wings, bright, tight smiles and warm eyes. I nodded at them and got center stage, just in time for the lights to come up.

"Phoenix, Arizona, we are Approaching Grace. Are you ready to find it?" Our slogan passed my lips without me noticing. The roar of the audience shook the stage and I dug my feet in. The adrenaline came over me and, suddenly, I was *there*. "Let's do this thing."

The band kicked in with "Like a Memory" and the crowd was in it. I used the energy of the crowd to ignore the pang of worry in my heart. I focused on their faces to ignore the feeling of being watched by my bandmates.

Despite everything, we were as tight as ever. We went from song to song with the grace and ease of a prima ballerina. The music reverberated and escaped into the evening air from under the canopy of the amphitheater. And, oh yes, it felt like it was about ten billion degrees on the stage, but that just meant everyone was hot and sweaty together, an intimate betrayal of one of our weakest moments shared with thousands of strangers. We bounced through the show, almost gleefully. (Later, concert reviewers would call it one of our best shows ever, though that viewpoint was undeniably colored by what happened next).

"All right, all right. I want to dedicate this next song to all of you out there who have never had a song dedicated to you. And I also want to dedicate it to our drummer, the heartbeat of our band, Amy Collins."

I turned around and gestured towards Amy. Her face dropped in a mixture of shock and anger. I'd been doing this introduction for months now, but she was still surprised. Amy stood up from behind her drums and waved at the audience before sitting back down.

I got back on the mic. "This is 'You Know'." I gestured to Tom to start the song and he hesitated. I motioned again and he sighed, then started.

You know I've known a thousand loves
You know I've been a thousand homes
And heard a thousand love songs,
But you know it's nothing like this—

The song staggered in as David joined Tom and me. At the chorus, Amy kicked in with the drums. At that moment, everything was as perfect as it had ever been. We were in sync, working together in that sacred act of live performance. I went over to David and threw my arm around his neck. He relaxed into my touch, before jolting awake and wiggling out of my embrace. When I looked at him for that unspoken explanation, he kept his head down, and his eyes glued to the neck of his bass, a move he hadn't needed to do since we started playing. Stepping away, I went to find Tom.

He was in front of his pedal board, changing his settings to start his guitar solo. I knelt in front of him, sitting in (only partially) faux reverence of his guitar glory, as I always did. Once I was in position, I scanned his face. My eyes lingered on his clenched jaw and tightly pressed lips. Without looking at me, he gave a single shake of his head before walking off. The crowd lost their mind as he took his solo to the other side of the stage. The notably shy guitarist was playing directly to the audience.

I pulled myself off the ground and went back to center stage. Unsure of what to do, I grabbed my tea off of the drum riser and took a sip. With my back to the audience, I waited for Amy to see me. As Tom's solo ended, I was washed in her gaze. I sang,

You know I love you,

like a river loves the rocks,
like a monster loves the dark,
like no one has ever loved me.
You know, you know.

Amy bared her teeth at me like a wild animal. That's when I finally realized that the streaks on her face were tears, not sweat. My heart dropped, but the screams of the audience tore at me, and I turned away.

I was holding the many hands of the hydra that was the audience when I sang the final lines of the song. And as that final declaration of love tumbled out of my mouth, I heard silence. Through the roaring crowd noise, I noticed the distinct lack of the ending drum fill.

Time itself slowed down. The open air of the amphitheater became tight and unwelcome. The giant stage seemed to shrink, bringing Tom and David unbearably close to me. The drums behind me were empty. With four songs left on the setlist, Amy had walked off the stage. My vision was filled with TV static as I watched David and Tom follow in her footsteps.

Alone on the stage, I stood. The audience persisted behind me, the tidal waves of their confusion and anger and love hitting my back as I walked off into the wings on the other side of the stage.

Jason ran past my seat on the hallway floor.

"I'm right here," I called. I slotted my head between my knees and my chest as his shoes squealed back to me. In the gap of my elbow, I saw those same chatty shoes. Black tennis shoes, scuffed from running down hallways just like this on the way to fix broken bands just like mine.

"Sam, what the hell happened out there?!" The angry

shouts of the audience had subsided and were now replaced by Jason's voice.

I shook my head in its cradle. "I tried to fix a problem and just made it bigger."

"Understatement of the century, Samantha. I have Amy coming to me saying she quits, and the other two saying they won't work in this kind of tense environment."

I scoffed. "That's rich coming from the guys. All they've ever done is argue."

"Now is not the time for jokes," he barked.

"I know!"

Jason sighed, and for a moment I thought he was going to leave. Instead, I heard his windbreaker sliding against the wall as he sat next to me on the linoleum. He put his arm around my shoulders and pulled me into his side. I wanted to fight him off, to tell him I was fine, but I didn't. I wasn't all right. *I might never be all right again.* A sigh shuddered out of me and I collapsed into his arms.

"I've already dealt with the venue, so we're clear there. The good thing is that there are only five dates left on this leg, so you don't lose too much." There was a pause. "I guess waiting to book the next leg was the right move."

I lifted my head onto my knees and stared at the name-clad wall, all of the logos and autographs of years of great artists were staring back at me as I spoke.

"Do you think this is really the end?" I felt him nod. "After all this time, after coming so far, we have taken ourselves out when no one else could."

The hallway was reduced to the sound of shuffling feet, rolling equipment, and unintelligent chatter as I sat there with Jason.

Approaching Grace was over.

Leaving Home Ain't Easy

THE AFTERMATH of the explosion involved logistics I had never considered. A crew of twenty people had to be laid off, but not before Mike drove the bus, and me, back to Fortress Grace. The others had vanished the moment they walked off the stage, so that left me to take on the responsibility of the bus.

The ride home was practically silent. To call it a ghost town would be both an understatement and a truth, considering the dead onboard now outweighed the living four to two. Mike didn't ask questions, seeming to connect the previous weeks of tension to my solitary return. The majority of the trip was spent in the back lounge, drifting through a dream as Joey and Ronnie went through movies like toilet paper. Blades' arms were wrapped around me, asking no questions, pushing no boundaries. When I first came back, though, there had been many questions.

"We saw everything. What are you going to do?" Mark asked, frantic.

"Nothing." I collapsed on the back couch.

"What do you mean? You have to fix this!" Joey said.

"How do you fix this?" I gestured to the empty bus. "I tried to prevent this exact thing.... Actually, that's a lie." My arms dropped. "I didn't even realize this could happen. I didn't know it was that bad."

Blades sat beside me and I rested my head on his shoulder. "Well, what are you going to do now?" he gently prodded.

"I'll figure that out when we get home."

"But what about—"

I jolted up in my seat. "I swear to God, Joey—" My voice caught in my throat and then the tears started. The very foes I had so keenly eluded to this point came rushing down. I was ambushed, caught at the end of a one-way street, and simply taken over.

That stopped the questions for a while.

By the time we got home, a few days later, I was feeling a bit better. That was short-lived, however.

It all started when I unlocked the door and gasped, "We've been robbed." The living room laid ransacked. Gone were the pillows and blankets, the wall decor, and the rug. The kitchen was barren of its small appliances. Mark and the guys trailed in behind me as I ran upstairs. My room was in perfect shape, with the exception of one thing. In the middle of my bed sat a plain black frame with that damned photo.

As the veil of confusion threatened to resettle over my eyes, it was suddenly ripped away when I stepped into Amy's room. It was empty, as were Tom's and David's. We hadn't been robbed at all. They had all moved out.

One of the benefits of having a Grammy Award–winning album and a sold-out tour was the money. And, as I could now attest, few things boost sales like drama. It's second only to dying, it would seem. Within a week of coming home, I was already moving out.

I looked for a place big enough to accommodate having a band of spirits following me around. They didn't need bedrooms, so I just told the realtor I was looking to host a lot of big parties, a lie that would give me the space I needed. I also needed space for a studio.

Looking back on all these years of touring across the country, and even the world, I've realized that there are very few places that I feel uneasy in. Sure, I can get a little lost or feel a little out of place, but I am a quick settler. No matter if I know no one, I have always been able to fake it till I make it. Hell, I practically made a career out of it. Perhaps that's what made moving out of Fortress Grace so difficult as, for the first time in years, I was totally out of my element.

I set my bags down in the grand front hall of my new house. The moving company had finished their work early yesterday, but I decided to give the place a bit to settle before moving in, myself. The house was big, to say the least, but it was made even bigger by the fact that I was the only real occupant. Everything around me was my own. The art was my art. The furniture was my furniture. There was no assigning areas to different people, no designation of chores. Everything was mine.

And I hated it.

"Woah Sam! This place reminds me of the house I bought in Malibu in eighty-eight," Joey said, as the group appeared within the foyer around me.

I jolted a bit, but sighed in relief. "Well, at least you guys are here. I was afraid for a moment that there'd be some sort of supernatural reason you couldn't apparate in new buildings or something."

Mark seemed to chew on this thought for a moment before saying, "We showed up in that new venue you played at in Jersey."

"Oh yeah, you're right. I forgot about that," I said, trailing off as I went on an exploration of my new house. Beyond the foyer was a large living room with a connected kitchen and dining room. To the right of the foyer was a hallway that led to a few rooms, including a downstairs recording studio. To the left of the foyer was a series of hallways that led to a collection of bedrooms. I left the boys to examine the home theater (conveniently situated next to my music room) and went to see my new bedroom.

With my bags in hand, I started down the hallway, but the photos on the walls stopped me. Unlike the photos in the Fortress, the photos here were not of my friends, but rather of my family. There were also photos of me with other musicians, like when I met Evanescence, and famous figures, like when I met Michael J. Fox at a charity event. The photos didn't bring the joy that I thought they would when I picked them out. *Something voyeuristic about seeing yourself on your own walls.* I shook my head and continued down the hall, finally reaching my room.

The room was centered around a seemingly giant king-size bed done up in celestial print sheets and covers. In the corner was one of my pianos—the ease of access had been Mark's idea—and across from that was a classic ivory vanity. I set my bags to the right of the door and soon found myself staring at the ceiling from my new bed. *This is all my stuff. I bought it. But something's not right.* In the distance, I could hear the faintest sounds of the boys venturing back from their exploration of the west wing of the house. As the sounds diminished again, I sighed and shook my head . *What's wrong with you? How are you gonna drop two million on a house and then get pouty when you move in? Huh?* A chill ran down my spine and I climbed under the new, clean covers.

"This is a great place you've got here, Sam," Blades said, walking into my room.

I wiped off a few stray tears from my face and picked my head up to look at him. "Yeah, it's really something."

His face dropped and he quickly came over to me and sat on the bed. No indent was made on the bed. *New bed. Of course.* I started to cry in earnest now.

"Samantha, what's wrong?" he asked, his voice soft and gentle as if he didn't want to scare me off.

I shook my head. "It's nothing."

"It's clearly *something*. Come on. What is it?" His cold hand cupped my cheek and I couldn't help but lean into it.

"It's the house."

"What's wrong with it?"

I shook my head again, "It's not *the house,* it's just—it's just—" I heard myself start to blubber as I began to fall apart even harder.

Blades pulled me into a hug. "*Shh shhh shh.* I know," he said, rubbing my back. "It's not the house. It's the people. It's Amy." Her name broke the last vestige of my strength and I basically collapsed in his arms. He held me strongly and stroked my hair.

"It's not that I'm not grateful that you're here, I just—" The words tumbled out of my mouth.

"Sam." He pulled me off his shoulder and looked at me. "You lived with them for years. Your whole adult life, even. It's natural that you'd be upset. It's a new space. But, I think this will begin to feel like home soon."

Home.

I looked around my room again as Blades put his arms back around me and settled into the bed, still without making an indent. With him holding me, the room held a different quality. It didn't seem quite as new. *Maybe I* can *get used to this.* I nuzzled into Blades a bit, then looked at the room one more time before closing my eyes.

This could be home. One day.

Only the Lonely

ONCE I WAS SETTLED into my new house, I really didn't know what to do. Pretty much my whole life leading up to that point had been focusing on making Approaching Grace a household name. Now we had succeeded in that task, but the band was dead (well, not quite *dead* like Stadium, but close enough).

So, I decided to do what I do best. I started thinking and planning; scheming, you might even call it. With the help of Blades and the guys, I started to work on a new album. Kratter had backed out of our deal after the breakup, so I had no label, but that didn't matter. Independent album release was old hat to me. I had done it before and I would do it again. Even to this day, everything I release is through my own label, Phoenix Records.

Those first few years were hard, I will be the first to admit it. To the public eye, I had to be strong. No one was supposed to know just how much I missed being in the band. The message we put out at the end said that we had decided to split on amicable terms, because we all wanted to be able to pursue our own unique creative visions. Because of this, we would have to play nice with the public. In interviews, Amy couldn't tell people how I betrayed them and I couldn't say how they abandoned me. Nice and neat, as per the lawyers.

During that time, I was very lucky to have Stadium with me. Not only did they give me advice and help me write the album, as always, but they also gave me company. Going from a band to a solo act meant that I was suddenly all on my own. I had session musicians that I hired for the album and a backing band that I put together for touring, but it was different. We were friendly, but we weren't friends. I was their boss and they treated me like it. We weren't a family. That is not to say that I didn't love Sid, Tara, Bill, Odie, Dolly, Savannah, Briana, Zach, and all the others who've helped me through the years. I love them all dearly and I truly owe the success of my solo career to their endless work, insight, and talent.

But, I would be lying if I didn't say it was different. In fact, it was quite different.

It's done. I sat in the back of the bus, surrounded by a paradise of blankets. My new band, specifically put together for this tour, were on a new, second bus. I had played the entitled diva card and claimed a need for my own space, though it was really just to keep Stadium to myself. Looking around the living room, I set out to burrow myself into a fabric heaven. And then I let my mind wander.

The crowd tonight was solid. Not as big as...but great for just starting out on my own. My eyes flickered to the TV, which Joey had turned on earlier and since abandoned, and saw a movie I didn't recognize. As the sounds of the movie seemed to fade away, I allowed myself to get lost in thought. *I wonder what they're doing on the other bus? I wish there wasn't a second bus. If I could just talk to Amy, I could...* My hands clenched, unconsciously. *Absolutely not. She's the one who broke up the band. She is the reason I'm out here alone to begin with. She is why I'm alone—*

The realization hit me like a fly meeting a windshield. *I'm alone.*

My hand shot out to grab the remote and I muted the TV with a *click*. I paused. From the front, I could hear the slightest sound of my new driver, Robin, listening to the radio, but beyond that—nothing but the sound of the wind rushing past the bus. Not even the ghostly nonsense of Stadium stood to surround me because it was late and the guys had gone to rest a while ago.

Alone. Surrounded by people, but alone. I am truly, utterly alone for the first time in years. A shiver seemed to run down my spine.

Can I get you anything, Ms. Roland? Please follow this way, Ms. Roland. Let me fix that for you, Ms. Roland.

But no "Sam" no "Stevie Ray" no jokes that cross the line, or memories from another time. *I am alone out here.*

The dread that fell over me was like a smothering wave. I could feel the ocean water lapping at my face and filling my eyes. *What if I'm alone like this forever? Who can save me now that it's over?* My eyelids were clamped shut as if I were afraid of a monster standing in front of me. But there wasn't one there. That was the problem.

Suddenly, I felt the presence of firm, solid arms around me and I moved to shriek. The hand that lightly clamped over my mouth to prevent or possibly muffle that threatened scream belonged to Blades. My vision was filled with him as he held me close. He pulled his hand away and put it around my shoulder as he brought me to rest in the crook of his neck.

"Why are you here? I thought you were resting," I croaked out, not moving from my new post.

"I was, but I felt your fear." His voice was low, warm, as if full of sleep. *I suppose it is, kinda.* "What happened?"

I shook my head. "It's nothing. It's gone now," I said, burying my face in his hair, letting it shield me from the world.

I'm not alone. Not now.

Don't Let It End

NOW I HATE to end this story on such a somber note, but I'll do some explaining as to why I chose to end it here. This book I'm writing, this memoir, is a story about Approaching Grace. It's not about my solo career, because I simply didn't want it to be (and it would make this way longer than I could imagine anyone would ever want to read). So, instead I focused on us. I focused on the story of how we, in the face of insurmountable odds, became one of the biggest rock bands of the twenty-first century (that's what *Rolling Stone* said, not my words. I would rather prefer to point out that the twenty-first century hasn't ended yet, so calling us that is hasty, at best). It is also the story of how Stadium overcame death itself to help us achieve the epic highs that we did.

As many of you reading this may well know, the length of my solo career has now outlasted the amount of time that Approaching Grace was together and I'm likely just as well known for my songs now as I am the ones I wrote at twenty-two. Despite this, I have been watching for years as people have made stories and books and movies and documentaries about us, so I figured it was time for me to throw my hat into the ring and lay down some facts that may not be as well known to the public.

Just as a note, both David and Tom approved my writing of this book and told me to be as truthful as possible. With that in mind, I am here to say that I tried my best. As for Amy, I don't know what she'll think. I haven't talked to her since that day in Arizona. But, I can only hope that, if she reads this, my words will not open old wounds and make them scar.

Now, if you truly want to learn more about my solo career, I apologize for leading you this far without giving you what you so desire. But, as the philosopher Jagger once said, "You can't always get what you want."

Epilogue

Now at the end of the book, Sam drew a shaky breath. She looked up at the four men around her, all still clad in leather and glitter and huge hair, all still surrounded in smoke, all still here. Trying to hold it together, she let her finger dance under the ink on the page.

"I will always be thankful for the life I got to live in exchange for the lives they lost. The members of Stadium never owed me or my friends anything. They definitely didn't owe us mentorship or, more importantly, friendship and love. For the past twenty-five years, these guys have helped us in ways never thought imaginable, and that's not just because of their 'special situation.'"

The phrase, coined by the guys themselves, caused Ronnie to chuckle, though he did not meet her eyes when she paused. The new silence was filled by the sound of a flipping page and she continued reading.

"Without these wonderful people, I'm not so sure Approaching Grace would've ever found the audience that it did. We owe so much to them. *I* owe so much to them. And so, to end this book, I will give my thanks to Stadium, the band that broke every barrier for us."

Her voice faltered on "us," shaking the S like a branch in a thunderstorm. Mark grabbed her hand, his cold grip intending to give her strength, but his small smile made it all feel more bittersweet.

"Samantha." *Always Ronnie with the full names.* She looked at his face, his eyes forever covered by his long bangs, letting just the tiniest bit of brown peek out. "It's okay. We've had a good run. Now it's time to let us go."

She closed her eyes, ready to shake her head, ready to deny him, ready to keep them all to myself, but she nodded instead and continued.

"First, to the one who never called me 'Sam,' who taught me the importance of a strong bass line, who told me that the best way to cook eggs was over easy, who helped me realize that I do have something to say and that the world should hear it. To Ronnie, thank you." With the words, Ronnie began to fade away, turning transparent before finally disappearing, leaving just the faintest hint of fog behind.

It actually worked.

Before she could choke on the air, she heard herself continue speaking. "Next, to the guy who was obsessed with Laffy Taffy, the one who told Amy that she had been tuning her drums wrong this whole time..." Joey's head shot up at the comment, realizing it was his turn. "To the one who, upon realizing that he could touch living people, immediately head-butted David, to the one who encouraged me more than anyone else." He was vibrating in his seat. "To Joey, thank you."

"Thank you, Sammie Davis! Joey has left the building!"

She laughed as he faded away, though the sound died on her tongue as soon as he was fully gone. She cleared her throat and looked at the two men left.

Mark nodded at her. "You're ready. You can let us go."

She nodded, "To the man who helped me grow my voice in insane ways, the one who taught me solid song structure and the importance of strong choruses, and who told David that the white streaks made him look more like an idiot than a star." His lips turned up into a smirk. "To Mark, thank you." Mark took her hand and kissed the top of it lightly before smiling into the abyss.

Sam closed the book, "Blades—"

"Sam—"

"I can't let you go like this—"

"Yes, you can and you have to." The air hung heavy. He cocked the hat on his head back, giving her a better look at his face, those blue eyes still twinkling over his blue-tinged lips.

"No, I don't. Who says that you have to leave?"

"Sam, we've been over this." He reached out to her, but she flinched away. "I'm tired, Sam. It's time for me to move on to whatever there is out there."

"I'm older now than you'll ever be," Sam said, softly. "I've spent more of my life with you than you ever spent alive. I don't know how to live without you." She felt those threatening tears start to make their entrance.

"You did it before, Star. You can do it again."

She stood up, tossing the all-important book on the couch. "But why should I? Is there even a point to all this without love, without you?" His cold arms pulled her into a hug, a kiss ghosting the top of her head.

"Don't say that, Sam." He pulled me away from himself and looked me in the eyes, "I swear, if I see you any sooner than I'm supposed to, it will not be pretty."

She sniffled at the half-baked threat. "How am I supposed to live without you?"

His familiar smile fell into position, soft and sweet. "You'll find a way. My clever girl, you always find a way. You're ready.

It's your time to shine, without us. Without all of this"—he gestured to the book—"baggage that you've been carrying for so long. He handed her the book. "Now, the sooner it's over with, the sooner it will stop hurting."

Sam took it from his hands and flipped to the last page. Blades moved behind her, putting his arms around her waist and his head over her shoulder.

"To the man who showed me ghosts are real, the one who calmed me when I cried, who told me I was enough. To the one who would scold me for not laughing at his jokes, who would tell me how well I did and I'd actually believe him, who I trusted more than anyone else. To the guy who taught me how to love and be loved. To Blades, thank you for loving me."

Sam closed the book and exhaled, and when she turned around, he was gone. They were all gone.

Sam could barely see through the tears she had in her eyes. She had felt alone before, after the band broke up, after she moved out, when she went on tour for the first time, and so many other times. But now she was *alone*. No voices bouncing down the corridors. No one to sneak up on her. There was no one. And so Sam did the only thing she could think of to do, that unspeakable thing that Mark and Blades had convinced her to do.

The phone rang a few times before she answered. "Hello?"

"They're gone."

"Who is this? And what could you possibly want at this hour?" The voice was groggy with sleep and irritation.

"Amy, they're gone."

"Samantha?" Amy asked, astounded.

After all these years, Sam had finally called her. As the shock from hearing Sam's voice wore off, the words hit her. And, of course, she understood. "Sam, I'm so sorry."

The words wrapped around her like a hug, like an old pair of shoes. Sam allowed herself to settle into Amy's voice.

"What are you going to do now?"

The question was there, just as Sam knew it would be. All these years apart couldn't erase decades of friendship. She wiped her nose on her sleeve and spoke the words she had practiced with Blades.

"I want to put the band back together."

About the Author

Hailey Ezzell sings and plays keyboard (among other instruments) for the Florida-based band Stone Lace, which performs a wide mix of music from the 1970s to today.

She also writes original music under her own name, including "Keep Coming Back," which was inspired by this novel. Ezzell's music is available on all streaming platforms.

Ghost Writers is her first novel.

www.ingramcontent.com/pod-product-compliance
Lightning Source LLC
Chambersburg PA
CBHW021714190726
48289CB00008B/2519